Wolf Walkers:
The Ambassador

ISBN: 9798319432629

Independently published

About the Author:

JL Thompson is a mother of four incredible kids, a wife, a professional tech nerd, and a pretty boring human in general. Thank goodness for books, specifically fantasy, romantasy, and dark romance, because the real world is 50 shades of beige.

JL, also known as Janine, is almost always working on a new book and will be focusing on the Wolf Walkers world for the foreseeable future.

Stay tuned for more contemporary romantasy from her.

Wolf Walkers

Book 1:
The Ambassador

JL Thompson

PROLOGUE

These boys are so energetic today. How in Luna's name am I going to get them settled in for bed?

"Bo, Jasper," I yell after the quickly moving boys.

They have been running around the outside of the house chasing my poor hens for the better part of the evening. It'll be a wonder if I get any eggs for the rest of the month.

Just then, my rooster, Gerald, jumps onto Jasper's back from the side porch railing. In his fright, the boy shifts into his wolf and takes off across the lawn toward the woods.

"Great," I mutter to myself. "Now I have to track a rogue pup."

Both boys turned 5 this year, and Jasper has just started shifting. No surprise that he's an early bloomer, with his mother and father being the strongest wolves in the realm.

As I untie my apron, I see Bo fall to the ground. Hairs are sprouting all over his neck and arms.

"Oh, for Luna's sake," I yell and dart down the porch steps to my baby boy.

"Jasper," I yell. "You need to come back to me, Bo needs you, he's shifting for the first time."

It's a long shot, but if the boy hears me, he might be able to gain his senses enough to shift back to his human form and help his best friend. These two are like peas in a pod and have been since they first met as tiny babes.

If I didn't know better, I would swear they were twins separated at birth.

Reaching my son, I turn him to face me, expecting to see pain or fear in his little baby face. Instead, I see his father's strong determination staring at me.

"It's ok, baby," I say, running my hand along the top of his head. Half of his hair is gone and replaced by the softest chestnut fur I have ever felt.

"Just relax, baby," I continue. "Let the shift happen. It's OK, I'm right here with you."

Glancing toward the tree line, I can see Jasper's golden blonde hair and tiny, awkward body running towards me. It's hard to believe that these two rambunctious little cherub-faced hellions will become the two strongest wolves in the realm someday.

Jasper is close now, and I can see the joy on his face at the sight of his friend.

"Come on then," Jasper squeals at Bo. "Just say it, like inside of your brain. WOLF!"

I smile at the alpha guiding his friend. Turning back to Bo, I can see the concentration in his eyes, and hear a tiny little whine escape him as he pushes through his first shift.

Sure enough, after only another few moments, Bo starts shifting more. Before I am ready, but not a moment too soon, my baby boy is standing in front of me as the most adorable little brown wolf pup.

"Good job, boys," I say, looking between the two of them. "Now, who wants to go for a short run before bed?"

Jasper shifts back into his pup form, and I follow, shifting into my dark grey wolf. The two pups weave through my legs, walking right under my belly with ease.

I start the trot toward the tree line and let their little legs work hard to keep up with me. It only takes about 15 minutes before I am carrying both pups with my maw.

Striding back to the side porch, I set the boys down and shift back to my human form. I grab a robe from just inside the door and a couple of my husband's shirts for the boys.

When I turn back, I can see that Jasper is back to his human form and is kneeling next to Bo's wolf.

"Just say it in your brain," Jasper is telling him. "Hoomun."

Luna willing, these two will always be this tight. Together, they'll be able to tackle any obstacle.

"OK, boys," I say. "How about a snack and then a story before bed? Just as soon as Bo gets his hands back, it's blueberry muffins and warm chocolate milk for you both."

The key to a successful first shift…the right motivation. With a blueberry muffin and chocolate milk on the line, Bo slowly starts to take on his human features, and in under a minute, my baby boy is standing before me with a huge smile on his face.

"What story?" Bo asks, taking the way-too-large button-down shirt from my hand. "Can it be the one about the lost goddess?"

Ushering the two boys into the house, I say. "Sure, baby, I can tell you the story of Datura, again."

40 years later...

"A *human*," I yell. He had to be out of his damned mind to think this was a good idea. "Are you insane? You can't bring a human, a human *woman* no less, to live here with us!"

"Why not?" he counters. His tone is casual and calm. He might as well have been discussing dinner choices.

"Let's start with the fact that our existence has been a secret since the first Vikings roamed the Earth," I say, pacing in front of his desk.

He smiles at me, smiles. "Other humans inside the government already know about us. Bringing a human ambassador into the community is an easy olive branch for us to extend to them. It's not like we can buy them off with Faerie magic. If we want to keep them from demanding that we open our borders or give them rule of our communities, then we have to show them that we have nothing to hide."

"You are making my points for me," I say. How can he not see this for what it is, human spy infiltration? "Humans fear anything that is more powerful than they are. Fear turns into aggression, and the next thing you know, every community in the world is surrounded by human troops in a coordinated attack to wipe us out."

He stands up and walks around to the front of his desk. Stopping right in front of me, he grabs both of my hands in his. For a moment, I'm struck by how much larger his hands are than mine. When did he get so big?

The contact between us eases some of the tension in me. It's in our nature to crave physical contact, especially when we are upset.

Looking me directly in the eyes he says, "Mom, you watch too much TV. The council and I have discussed this for months. We researched the potential candidates thoroughly. This woman is exactly who we need to liaise on our behalf with the humans. It's a new world out there, and we need their cooperation to stay hidden and protect our people. Trust me."

PART ONE:

Ellie

Chapter One

"Are you ready for tonight?" Caroline asks me with an exaggerated fake smile. In just five short hours, our entire office staff will be forced to sit through yet another celebratory dinner party touting the outstanding diplomatic prowess of our fearless leader, Ambassador James D. Morris IV.

It will be hour after hour of toasts and speeches, claps on the shoulder, and pats on the back. I like to think of it like a political prom night, complete with a jackass Prom King and overly perky Prom Queen.

You would think that Morris would at least have given us the day off. Instead, we are stuck in the conference room of his Washington, D.C. office. It's not even a nice conference room. While his personal office is outfitted with a large mahogany desk, fancy couches, and absurdly expensive chairs, the conference room contains an old particleboard table with a faux wood grain finish and the cheapest office chairs you can buy. I wouldn't be surprised if this furniture came from one of those online yard sale sites.

"I'm still hoping for food poisoning, or maybe a mild stroke," I say back to her with an equally fake smile. We both giggle, despite being half serious about preferring a stroke over suffering through, yet another, of the Ambassador's congratulatory dinner celebrations.

"I don't understand why we even have to go to these stupid things," I say to her, with a little bit more whine in my voice than I had intended.

"Are you serious?" Caroline says, turning away from the pile of documents she is categorizing for archive, and facing me with her entire body. She puts her hands on her hips and raises her eyebrows at me. She looks like the stereotypical sassy co-worker from every sitcom. "Without us, especially you, Morris wouldn't be able to answer a single question about the Royal Council, let alone the damn treaty that he 'single-handedly' negotiated."

I know she's right. We all know it. We busted our asses and worked for years to gain the trust of the royals and their council members. We put our safety on the line and worked for months to bring the rebels to the negotiation table. All the while, Morris sat in a giant leather executive's chair back in D.C. and ate at 5-star restaurants every night.

We secured a peace treaty between the rebels and the royal council, resumed trade with the United States, and negotiated the release of the rebels' hostages, seven of whom were American cargo ship crewmen. Morris flew in after everything was said and done. He stuck around for a few hours to meet the Royals, then posed for photos around a big oak desk and hightailed it back to D.C.

"I wish he would just let me make him note cards or something," I say, in what I hope is a less bratty tone.

Caroline shakes her head. "Girl, the Secretary of State will be there. So put on your fancy dress, get your hair and face done up, and schmooze the shit out of that man. These parties are brutal, but they're the best way to get in front of the real decision-makers. It's the best place to audition for the next big assignment. Show the rich white guys that you are the one who makes it happen."

She is absolutely right. Only, I don't care about moving up the ladder. I honestly don't care that Morris is always stealing credit for my work.

"I love my job, but I hate the politics, Car," I say, while rolling my eyes. "Political dinners and ass-kissing are worse than diarrhea in the desert. I just want to do my job and make the world a better place. I don't care who gets the credit. Morris can ride my successes right into a fancy new office, I'll be at the embassy working on the next conflict."

"While I admire your whole 'Mother Theresa' thing," Caroline says with a laugh, "some of us like shiny cars and designer bags. So, if you don't want the credit, you can give it right to me. I'll gladly take that man's office and salary on your behalf."

I can't help the giggle that escapes.

※

Two hours of hair and makeup has me looking like some kind of cable news reporter. Don't get me wrong, the stylist did an amazing job, and I look great. I just prefer to keep my look simple and natural. False eyelash extensions, perfectly contoured and highlighted features, and carefully crafted curls are just not my style. I am much more of a plain Jane type. Having a perfectly average face, pale hazel eyes, medium blonde shoulder-length hair, mildly tall at 5'8", and only slightly above average muscle tone keeps me from standing out in a crowd. I am a casting director's dream background actor, attractive enough but certainly not star quality.

Everything about me has been designed by the gods to blend in.

That is, except for on banquet nights.

As Ambassador Morris's right-hand woman, I am expected to look and act the part of a high-society political powerhouse. My designer gown is professionally tailored, while my hair, makeup, and perfume are of the highest quality. Or so I'm told. I'm more of a boots-on-the-ground girl than a fancy banquet girl, but it all comes with the job.

Tonight's little shindig has me donning a heavily beaded black halter-neck gown with a deep V in front and an open back. The mermaid cut hugs my frame and shows off the lines of my tightly toned body nicely. I am fiercely devoted to my yoga routine and take pride in my body. So, if I'm forced to wear a fancy dress, why not show it off just a little?

I really do look the part.

I never understood why this was such a big part of the job. My abilities as a diplomat have nothing to do with how much my dress cost, or what shade my lipstick is. The whole banquet is an absolute waste of time, money, and energy. The only good thing about these events is the mandatory car service. At least none of the flying monkeys will be driving home drunk tonight.

My driver pulls up to the front of the conference center and a valet opens my door for me while extending a hand to help me from the backseat. I roll my shoulders, take a deep cleansing breath, and grasp his hand. Time to plaster on my well-practiced polite smile.

Having been raised by diplomat parents, I'm an accomplished fake smiler. I might despise these formal ass-kissing parties, but that doesn't mean I'm not a pro at handling them.

Really, the skillset isn't so different from dealing with a hostile foreign leader. Smile, nod, repeat back what they last said to make them feel like they have your undivided attention, and play to their ego by asking simple questions.

Moving through the cocktail area, I see many faces that I recognize from previous events, and even some people I have worked alongside on previous assignments. Caroline and two of our office admins are by the bar waiting for drinks. I start heading toward them when I feel a strange sensation, like someone is watching me from the shadows. Looking around, I immediately spot Lawrence Simmer, the office misogynist, staring at me like some sort of predatory cat.

Quickly, I turn away and head straight for the bar. Dealing with dear old Larry will definitely require some sort of fruity vodka-based beverage.

As I order my drink, I can see Larry making his way to me from the corner of my vision. He and Morris are old college friends, but rumor has it that Larry has some sort of scandalous photo or video of Morris. If not, there is no way he would risk his office's reputation on someone as sleazy and underhanded as Captain Larry Grab-ass.

"Wow," Larry's greasy voice sounds from right behind my right ear. "You really should dress up more in the office. In that dress, with the makeup and all, you look absolutely fuckable. I like this dress better than that piece of shit you wore at the last thing. Shows off your ASS-ets better."

Gritting my teeth, I turn to the side and take a step back. I like to keep as much distance as possible between Larry and myself.

I steel my face into a saccharine sweet smile.

"Well, *Larry*, I don't give a shit what you find attractive," I say in a quiet but super friendly voice. "Don't you have a date to bother? Surely there's at least one working girl left in this city who will still put up with you. Or are you blacklisting your way through Virginia now?"

Larry's face turns red with anger. His masculinity, or lack thereof, is such an easy target.

"You got a smart mouth on you, little girl," Larry says, not even bothering to hide the fact that he is staring at my breasts. "Seems to me you just need a good…"

Larry is suddenly cut off by a large man sliding up beside me.

"There you are," the stranger says as he lightly touches my elbow.

Turning to face Larry, he says, "I'm sorry. I interrupted you. Please, continue. I can't wait to hear where you are going with that."

Larry stares at the large stranger for a moment with his mouth still hanging open with the unspoken words.

The strange man lifts his eyebrows at Larry, inviting him to continue speaking. Larry just closes his mouth and gives the man a small nod.

"Well, if you're done, I guess you don't mind if we go. People to meet, hands to shake. You know the deal." The stranger motions for me to walk in front of him, in the opposite direction from Larry, and gives me a sly wink. So sly that I'm not sure if I really saw it, or if my mind is playing tricks on me.

We stride away from Larry shoulder to shoulder, or at least shoulder to mid-bicep. The man is unusually tall. Once we are safely out of Larry's earshot, he leans toward me slightly and introduces himself as Bo Ragnulf.

"Nice to meet you, Mr. Ragnulf," I say with my customary diplomatic politeness.

We reach a small stand-up table near the edge of the cocktail area and stop to place our drinks down.

"Please, call me Bo," he says with a casual smile. "I'm sorry about jumping in there, I don't usually make a habit of butting into other people's conversations, but that guy was way out of line, if I didn't step in, then I wouldn't be able to look my mother in the eyes ever again."

While Bo is apologizing, I take the opportunity to survey him. He is broad-shouldered and built more like an action hero than a politician. He has short chestnut-colored hair, slightly longer on top than the sides. His strong jawline and perfectly straight teeth give him the look of coming from money. His eyes are bright and clear, and a peculiar color of light brown, fading to almost golden toward the pupil. It's like a sunburst in his eyes.

"There's really no need to apologize, Bo," I say with a slight laugh. "You can rest assured that I'm grateful for the save. I can handle Larry and his disgusting advances perfectly fine on my own, but I will treasure this memory. His face was priceless when you told him to continue. I honestly didn't know if he was going to blow his top or piss his pants."

"I don't know him, but I know his type." Bo continues. "Bullies are tragically predictable. It's none of my business, but how did you get tangled up with a guy like that?"

I spend the next few minutes explaining where I work, and how Larry torments the entire female staff. "Thankfully, he mostly stays here in D.C. with my boss, Ambassador Morris, so we only have to deal with him when we come back for events like this, or they come for a visit to the embassy."

I can see the spark of interest on Bo's face when I mention that I work for Morris. Apparently, this was the opening he was looking for. It's all starting to come together now. Playing the hero, chasing Larry away from me, it's all in hopes that I will get him in to see Morris for some reason.

Judging by his size, I assume he is involved in some sort of private security. It makes sense. He is too athletic to be a politician; they favor a smaller, less threatening build. His tux is far too nice to be rented, and it has certainly been tailored to his frame. Plus, he is clearly comfortable in a room full of powerful politicians, foreign dignitaries, insanely wealthy businessmen, and even a few celebrities. This guy is no stranger to black-tie events.

I'm sure that I seemed like an easy target to such a good-looking man. I can't say that I blame him for targeting me. Women like me have probably been fawning over him since his teens. He was almost certainly the captain of his high school sports team, and definitely bagged the head cheerleader. I'm sure he expects a plain girl like me to fawn over him and thank my stars that such a handsome man wants my attention.

Sorry, my guy, this isn't my first rodeo. We spend some time chatting, and he's a surprisingly decent conversationalist. I find that I am actually enjoying his company. I don't expect, or really even want, anything to come of it. At the very least, his presence will keep Larry away.

As the evening creeps closer to the formal banquet part, I decide that I better move things along. No use pretending that this is something other than an attempt to get into an ambassador's office.

"So, Bo, what kind of work do you do?" I ask.

"Me," he says with a half-grin. "I guess you could say I'm a local politician and businessman."

"Really," I say, somewhat surprised by the local politician part, but not the businessman part. "I don't think I have seen you around, no offense, but you kind of stand out amongst the political types. Where are you located?"

Bo explains that he is from Oregon and is only in D.C. for some meetings. He spends the next half hour asking me about my work. The normal stuff: do I like it, why did I choose this path, and don't I want to settle down with a family? They always ask that one.

"My parents were both diplomats," I explain to him. "I grew up in embassies all over the globe. I learned about all different cultures and experienced the different hardships that exist throughout the world. It wasn't easy for us, traveling all the time and never really calling any one place home. But I decided at an early age that I wanted to follow in my parents' footsteps. Their work really made a difference in the world, and I knew that I would never be able to accept anything less than that from a career."

"Wow," Bo tilts his head to the side slightly before continuing. The move reminds me of a pitbull dog. "That was a great answer. I'm guessing that you've had a lot of practice with that one. And here I thought that my conversation skills were top-notch. I guess I'm not as original as I thought."

I laugh but nod yes. "I do get that one a lot. Being a single woman in her 30s, everyone assumes that I'm just waiting for Mr. Right to come along so that I can settle down, buy a big house, and have some kids. And there is nothing wrong with that, but I love what I do, and travel is a necessary part of it."

"It must be lonely," he says in a somber tone. Then immediately says. "I'm sorry, I don't mean any disrespect. It's just that I grew up in such a close-knit community. I can't imagine always saying goodbye to the closest people around me. There must be a way that you could save the world and still build a life for yourself surrounded by people who love you."

I am taken aback by his sudden seriousness. He is either a very good actor, or he genuinely feels sad for me. I'm not exactly sure how to react. I want to be offended. Who is he to judge my life? I like my life. On the other hand, he really does look sincere. Before Bo and I can delve further into my lonely lifestyle, the wait staff informs us that guests are now being seated for dinner.

Saved by the dinner bell.

※

The waiter leads me through the dining room towards my assigned seat. I am surprised when we stride right by the table with Caroline and my other co-workers. Instead, we are headed towards the head table in the front of the room.

Casually, I close the gap between the waiter and myself. "Excuse me, I think you might have me confused for someone else. My name is Eloise Margrave. I usually sit with Caroline Harper."

The waiter gives me a contrite smile, "No ma'am, I was asked specifically to bring you to the head table for dinner tonight."

With a slight frown, I continue following the waiter to the head table. Who could have requested me at this table? Maybe Morris is worried that he'll have to answer more questions about the treaty. Larry can't be trying to sleaze his way to my side without Bo, the security man—at least I hope he isn't at the head table.

Thankfully, as we continue toward the front of the room, we stroll right past Larry.

Coming to my seat, I look around at the other diners who are already seated. The table is host to a handful of senators, Ambassador Morris, and, *wholly crap*, I am seated next to Secretary of State Allan Viktor.

Chapter Two

Secretary Viktor excuses himself from the table to stand at the small podium, he gives a short speech congratulating Morris on a job well done. Since I'm sitting right up front where everyone can clearly see me, I consciously remind myself not to roll my eyes at the praise Secretary Viktor is heaping onto Morris.

As the Secretary returns, dinner is served to our table. I have no idea why I am seated with the big boss tonight. Lord knows that I have no interest in being on the big man's radar, let alone the room full of ambitious backstabbers who are shooting daggers at me from every corner of the dining hall.

Luckily, Morris doesn't allow anyone at our table the chance to speak. He fills the time with his mind-numbing ramblings about how difficult the negotiations were and how dangerous the rebels could be, as if he had any idea. Until I met Morris, I had no idea that you could hero worship yourself.

Despite his blatant lies, and obnoxious self-promotion to the Secretary, I am thankful for Morris' uncanny ability to talk about himself non-stop for hours. I only have to interject on occasion to clarify details or "remind" him of someone's name or title.

He drones on and on, only pausing to flash his too-white, veneered teeth at us. His entire look screams family money. His side-parted, obviously dyed, gel-locked hair. His stylist leaves just a hint of grey showing at the temples. It looks great in photos, but not so much up close. Not to mention his overly manscaped eyebrows and fake-bake tan.

Dinner will be over soon, and I can disappear into the crowd once again. Not that I am afraid of the Secretary, I certainly have no reason to be. I'm just not interested in "playing the game." Plus, if Morris thinks that I am trying to steal his thunder, he will do everything in his power to blacklist me.

It won't matter to him, or anyone else, that he is the one stealing my thunder and that I am the one who actually did all the work. Anyone who stands in the way of an ambitious politician can count on trouble.

I don't need that kind of hassle in my life, and I don't want it. The undeniable Ms. Taylor Swift had it right when she said that congressmen use covert narcissism and disguise it as altruism.

Congressman/Ambassador, close enough.

I am almost home free. The staff are finally clearing the plates, and everyone is starting to stand up to return to the banquet area.

People begin to crowd around us, looking for their 15 seconds of fame with the Secretary. I am trying to politely excuse myself from the Pennsylvania Senator when Secretary Viktor makes his way over to me. *Crap.*

"Ms. Margrave," he says to me, extending his hand for a shake. "I was hoping to speak to you for a moment."

I plaster on my best professional smile and shake the Secretary's hand with a well-practiced balance of firmness and warmth. "Of course, Mr. Secretary, what can I do for you?"

"I would like to discuss a possible future assignment with you," he says, flashing me his dazzling campaign smile. "Let's discuss it in my office at 8 a.m. on Monday."

"Absolutely, sir," I say. I am slightly uneasy about the Secretary of State coming to me directly about an assignment, not to mention the in-person meeting in his office. Normally, assignments are handed down through the chain of command or via memos. Never have I been asked to meet with the Secretary directly.

"Fantastic," Secretary Viktor says. "I'll see you then, Ms. Margrave. And, if you will, keep this meeting confidential."

"No problem, sir." Now I'm really curious about the nature of this meeting and possible assignment. What could the SoS want with a young and relatively unknown diplomat? It's not like I have been lobbying for his attention or seeking out any high-profile positions.

And why doesn't he want anyone to know about the meeting? Is he going to fire me? Maybe the "potential assignment" is a misdirection to keep me from asking around. Surely, if there was a new assignment coming into our office, Morris would be the one to brief us on it.

Great, there goes the rest of my weekend. There's no way I'll be able to relax now. What if Morris has been talking bad about me to keep his secret that all his successes are from my work and not his own?

Or maybe, Larry finally caused a big enough issue that the Secretary is involved. What if he wants me to go on record saying that Larry is a good man who would never harass a woman? Could I do that? Could I sell my soul to keep my job? Oh boy, this weekend is going to require at least a gallon of banana and chocolate chip ice cream.

※

Monday morning, I am up by 5 a.m., though to be honest, I didn't really sleep much. This weekend passed by slower than any weekend in the history of weekends. I've decided that my newest life hack for extending the weekend is to pretend there is a mysteriously ominous meeting scheduled with my boss's boss every Monday.

Of course, this is assuming that I still have a boss after the mysteriously ominous meeting.

The trip to Secretary Victor's office takes about a half hour, but I leave by 7 a.m. to give myself plenty of time. There is no way in hell that I will be late to meet with the Secretary of State.

By 7:45 a.m., I am sitting in the waiting area of Secretary Viktor's office with a cup of chai tea from the coffee shop on the corner. The tea really only distracts my fidgeting hands. My anxiety over the nature of this meeting has my stomach in knots, and there is no way that I can actually drink the tea.

My mind is racing as I wait. Is this suit appropriate for the meeting? It's a light brown designer pantsuit with a cream-colored silk blouse. Am I too bland? Maybe I should have worn a skirt. But what if there really is an assignment and it is in a remote or underdeveloped area where designer clothing is completely inappropriate? Maybe I am overdressed.

Or maybe this is about Larry's harassment, and I am underdressed.

Ugh, how long have I been sitting here? It's only 7:52 a.m. Is the Secretary already here, or am I waiting for him to arrive? What if he didn't mean this Monday, what if I am supposed to be here next Monday? No, surely his assistant would have told me if I was here on the wrong day. Right?

At 7:55 a.m., the assistant's phone buzzes, and I nearly jump out of my skin at the sound. She picks up the call on her headset and simply says, "Yes, sir."

She hangs up the call and stands from her desk. Walking around to the front, she turns her attention to me. "The Secretary is ready to see you now," she says in a very singsong, rehearsed sort of way. I wonder how many times she has uttered those words in her career.

Standing, I follow her to Secretary Viktor's office door. She opens the door for me, and I step inside.

Immediately, I notice that there is another person in the room. A man sits in front of the Secretary with his back to me. He is broad-shouldered and casually dressed in an olive-green T-shirt, dark jeans, and dark brown boots. He is leaning back with his left ankle crossed over his knee and his arms casually draped on the armrests. He looks completely comfortable in the Secretary's guest chair.

Who the hell is this guy? He gives off a vaguely familiar feeling. Have we met before?

As I enter the office, both men stand.

"Ah, Ms. Margrave," The Secretary says, with another campaign-worthy grin, and motions to the chair next to the strangely familiar man. "Lovely to see you again. Please, have a seat. I believe you have already met Mr. Bo Ragnulf."

Secretary Viktor gestures to the man sitting across from him, and it hits me: It's the security guy/local politician from the party last Friday night. What the hell is he doing in the Secretary of State's office?

Both men remain standing, waiting for me to move to my chair. As I walk across the office to the waiting seat, Bo keeps his attention on my face. What is he looking for? Shock? Recognition?

If I thought my mind had been racing before, it's full-on Indy race day in there now. Still, I keep my face neutral. What the hell is this guy doing here? Was he setting me up for something on Friday? Who is this guy?

Pulling myself together, I turn to Bo and nod. In a cold, professional tone, I say, "Nice to see you again, Mr. Ragnulf."

Undeterred by my demeanor, he smiles warmly and responds, "Nice to see you too, Ellie. No need to be nervous, and please do call me Bo."

"I'm simply surprised, Mr. Ragnulf," I say. Turning away from Bo, I face Secretary Viktor. "Mr. Secretary, it's nice to see you as well."

I take my seat, and both men sit at the same time.

"I'm sure you are very curious about the nature of this meeting, Ms. Margrave," the Secretary starts. "So, I'll get right to it. Firstly, let me say that everything that we speak about in this room today is to stay 100% confidential. You are not to discuss this meeting or anything that we say in this meeting with anyone outside of this room, is that understood?"

I nod and say that I understand.

"I am well aware that Ambassador Morris is not skilled at his job and that, frankly, the man is useless as tits on a bull," Secretary Viktor says, shaking his head.

Despite my best efforts, I can't help the small smile that creeps across my face.

"So, imagine my surprise when he is suddenly reporting successful trade negotiations and signed treaties from all over his territory. It didn't take a genius to figure out that he was taking the credit for your hard work. But what struck me was that you simply sat back and allowed him to do it." The Secretary holds up his hands in an inquisitive gesture. "So, care to elaborate on that?"

I am so totally taken aback by the Secretary's words that for a moment, I say nothing at all. A sideways glance reveals a smirk on Bo's too-perfect face. That smug look is all I need to quickly recover. "It doesn't really matter who gets the credit, sir. I didn't pursue this career for accolades."

The Secretary nods and asks, "OK. So, if not for the accolades, then why? Travel? Or maybe you have your eye on something in the private sector?"

Still confused about where this is going, I shake my head. "No, sir, that's not it. I do the job because I believe in the work. My only agenda is to leave the world a better place. I grew up with diplomat parents, and I always knew that I would follow in their footsteps one day."

"Yes," Secretary Viktor says. "In preparation for this meeting, I looked into your background and learned that your parents were both diplomats and were, sadly, lost in an embassy bombing several years ago. I don't mean to be insensitive, Ms. Margrave, but I must ask, why would you want to go into the same line of work that killed your parents?"

"It's ok, sir. I've actually gotten this question a lot since I graduated college," I say, matter-of-factly. It isn't a lie; I have been asked this question countless times, and my answer has become well-practiced. "My parents believed in their work, and they knew the risks when they took that assignment. I can't hold the world responsible for the actions of a few."

The Secretary looks towards Bo and then back to me. "That's a very…progressive outlook, and I'm very glad you feel that way. The truth is, Ms. Margrave, that I have a very special assignment that I need a very special Ambassador for. This placement is above top secret and would require you to hide the true nature of your work. It means never telling anyone outside of the program where you are living or who you are working with. I'll be honest with you, your lack of living family and, shall we say, trim social circle, led me to believe that you could walk into this role seamlessly and maintain the necessary discretion."

I am stunned by his words. I must have misheard him or misunderstood what he was trying to say. What the hell is happening here?

"Wait, sir," I look from the Secretary to Bo and back again with wide eyes. "Can I just clarify? You are offering me a promotion to a top secret position?"

Chapter Three

For the remainder of the meeting with Secretary Viktor and Bo Ragnulf, the two men fill me in on as much as they can without divulging the sensitive details of the assignment.

As it turns out, Bo, the self-proclaimed local politician, is actually the leader of a sovereign nation community located within the continental United States. Few know of their existence, and even fewer have been inside their borders.

For 45 minutes, I listened intently as the two men discussed the assignment. The gist is that I would become the U.S. Ambassador to Bo's community and work with Bo to keep the community off the radar of the local government and law enforcement agencies.

Secretary Viktor looks directly at me while he speaks, perhaps he is trying to gauge my reactions. "The idea is that, on the outside, you would appear to be a normal Ambassador to a secretive, but normal sovereign community. Not unlike the Native American communities contained within our borders. You will file mundane reports about trade between the community and area companies. It will appear to anyone looking into your position that you have simply taken an entry-level Ambassador role. However, in truth, you will be read-in to a top secret program and report directly to me, and only when absolutely necessary. For the most part, you will work on your own and have free rein to do what you need to in order to assist Bo in keeping his community safe. You will also work with him and his council to address a number of issues that we can't get into yet. I need you to understand, before you agree to anything, that this is not a normal Ambassador role. Your duties *would* include acting as a liaison between the community and the United States government, but they will also go well beyond that."

I can't help but note the way the Secretary keeps using the word "normal." I would need to make people believe that it is a normal community, which implies that it is anything but normal. What could the big secret about this community be? How can they keep it a secret from everyone? Why do they keep it a secret?

I don't know enough about this assignment to make a decision just yet. Maybe if I understand why the Secretary wants me for the position, I can glean some insight into what they really want from me.

"Sir," I say when he is through, "Can I ask what made you come to me for this assignment?"

Secretary Viktor smiles. "For one thing, you are very good at asking seemingly innocent questions that reveal hidden answers."

OK, I'm busted. I try to smile as innocently as possible and feign ignorance. It is always better for people to think you are dumb. Since most people are eager to believe that they are smarter than you, they take the bait and reveal their secrets while trying to prove their intelligence.

I learned this trick from superheroes. Get the villain talking, and before you know it, they have revealed their entire secret plan.

Secretary Viktor isn't falling for it but surprisingly answers anyway: "This role is essentially off the books. There will be no fanfare, no upward advancement opportunities, and no obvious political weight. Only a handful of high-ranking individuals know the nature of this program. The person who ultimately takes this role will need to be in it for the greater good. They will need to be able to leave D.C. for extended periods of time without having to explain why or where they are going. This assignment is a commitment of the highest order. It will be more than a career decision; it will be the rest of your life."

I lean my weight against the back of the chair. That was more than I was expecting. It appears that my lack of political ambition has landed me in the Secretary of State's hot seat. Who'd a thunk it?

"Sir, can I ask how many candidates you are considering and how long I have to reflect on this?" I ask.

Secretary Viktor looks to Bo, who nods so slightly that I am not sure if I actually saw it.

"You are the only candidate at this time, Ms. Margrave," he says. "As for your time frame, we would like you to spend this week working with Bo and meeting some of his advisors. We can reconvene next Monday at 8 a.m. to discuss your decision."

What in the actual hell is going on? I'm the only one they are talking to. This is a life-long position; what does that even mean? I'm going to spend the week with Bo and his advisors, but where? Am I going to be sequestered? What about my job with Morris?

"Sir," I say, "What about my position with Ambassador Morris? If I'm to work with Bo this entire week, I will need to tell him something."

Secretary Viktor calls out to his assistant through his desk phone. The woman appears almost immediately in the doorway. "Please let Ambassador Morris know that Ms. Margrave will be filling in for the Ragnulf Ambassador for the foreseeable future. Tell him that we will contact his office next Monday regarding her schedule and possible replacement."

Turning to me, the Secretary says in dismissal, "I will leave it to you two to work out the rest of the details for the week."

With that, we all stand and say our goodbyes.

As Bo and I walk out toward the street, we decide to go to the coffee shop to set our plans for the week. I have no idea what he expects of me, but I need some answers.

I start forming a list of questions in my head. Will I be traveling with him to his community? Where did he say he was from at the party? I'm sure it was the West Coast, but was he being honest about it? What is he, some sort of King or something? How many people are we talking about, five, five hundred, five thousand? What kind of political leader wears jeans to the SoS's office?

Top secret locations and hidden communities…my head is spinning by the time we reach the coffee shop. I want to ask a million questions, but I know that Bo can't answer most of them until I am read-in to the program and given clearance.

As we sit down with our coffees at the back of the café, I decide to start at the beginning and get as much information out of Bo as I can.

"Let's start simple," I say. "What is the plan for this week? Are we traveling to your community, or am I going to meet with your people here?"

Having worked with all types of scary individuals over the last 7 years, I have become very good at hiding my anxiety. Even though my mind is racing, and questions are bouncing around my head like an out-of-control superball, I keep my tone even, and my words come out unrushed.

I don't really know Bo, and while I believe in the good of the world, I am not naïve. This man is the leader of a community large enough and important enough that he is granted access to the SoS. He is a powerful man, and he potentially holds my life in his hands. He will not see me squirm if I can help it. I never want to appear apprehensive or weak.

Externally, I am the picture of composed confidence.

Bo simply smiles at me as he stirs the cream and sugar into his coffee. He is sizing me up, waiting to see if I will cave into his silence and flounder to fill the gap in conversation.

I don't.

Instead, I return his gaze with an equally sweet smile and wait for his response.

"I am very impressed by you, Ellie," Bo says with a slight tilt of his head. I am beginning to realize that he does that when he is caught off guard. "Despite your nervousness, you appear completely calm."

"What makes you think that I'm nervous?" I ask.

Again, Bo smiles and lets my question hang for a moment before he says, "Your pulse is racing, eyes are dilated, and you are tapping your pinky on your cup in a rhythmic tempo. My guess is that it's a grounding technique for you. Something to focus on while you work to keep your breathing and speech tempered."

What? Who the fuck is this guy?

Is he some kind of CIA assassin or something? Am I going to live with a group of trained interrogators?

Calming breaths. I can handle this. He's just another politician, just a man. He's trying to rattle me, and I will not let him.

"I'm simply worried that I won't have time to pick my dress up from the dry cleaners if you are expecting me to board a plane this afternoon," I reply as coldly as I can.

Annoyingly, Bo lets out a small chuckle at my agitation. "I'm sorry, Ellie, I really didn't mean to offend you."

Seriously, who is this guy? Does he think he can play me like a fiddle because he has a nice smile? I am not some schoolgirl, and he is not the first attractive and powerful man to try this tactic on me.

I remain silent. I won't start this assignment off by giving Bo the upper hand in our exchanges. I asked a direct question, and I will not move on until he either answers it or plainly states that he will not answer it.

"OK, let's start over," Bo says, holding up his hands and showing me his palms in surrender. "I'm sensing a lack of trust from you, and I'm guessing that you feel a little deceived by me right now. So, I'll lay my cards on the table for you. Yes, I did seek you out at the party on Friday. No, I did *NOT* plan to 'white knight' you away from that dickhead at the bar. I honestly just wanted to meet and speak with you before you knew who I was. I needed to see if the Eloise Margrave that I read about on paper was the same in person. That's all. I promise."

Some of the tension leaves my body. Maybe I have been a bit suspicious of Bo, and therefore a bit annoyed by him as well. But I didn't bring any of that up. This guy must be a master at reading nonverbal cues.

Interesting.

I decide to change my approach. I grant Bo a smirk and visibly relax my posture before taking a long sip of my coffee. "I appreciate your honesty," I say with a little more warmth in my tone. "I had wondered if you were setting me up for something, or maybe trying to influence my decision by rescuing me from Larry and spending the rest of the cocktail hour flirting with me. Initially, I had assumed that you were planning to use me to get to Morris."

Bo nods and answers, "I promise, I had no plans to dominate your night. Our conversation was 100% natural, and by no means do I want you to feel like I'm trying to influence you in an unprofessional way. Any and all flirting was simply my natural inclination around an incredible woman. Now let's start this week off right. The only reason I asked for this week-long trial is so we can get to know each other a little. This isn't a normal assignment. Taking this job means becoming a member of my family. We need to be comfortable with each other and trust each other completely. So, we'll spend this week on your turf. We can meet with my advisors every morning at my hotel. Then, we'll have lunch, and you can ask me any questions you have about the morning session. Obviously, we can't get into anything classified, but there are plenty of other matters that we can address this week."

This guy is really starting to surprise me. Reluctantly, I admit to myself that I might actually like Bo. So far, he seems like the kind of man who faces things head-on and doesn't beat around the bush or deflect blame. These are qualities that I admire. It makes my job—and my life—much easier when someone is upfront and honest about what they need.

"That sounds great," I say. "Talking with your staff about some of the non-classified work they are doing can help me get a feel for your people. What can you tell me about your community?"

Bo raises his eyebrows and smirks; he is clearly happy with himself for breaking through my coldness. "I have lived there my whole life, and outside of our big secret and government structure, I can't think of anything that would set us apart from a normal city. Since you're the world traveler, why don't you ask me some questions, and I will answer as much as I can?"

"Fair enough," I say. "Let's start with the basic demographics. How many square miles, how many citizens, median income?"

Bo tells me that the borders are roughly 1,700 square miles, but most of that area is wooded. There are around 800,000 citizens, but not all citizens live within the borders. A central city houses around 300,000 people, another 250,000 live on the outskirts in smaller towns, 50,000 live in remote homesteads, and 200,000 live abroad.

"I can't reveal much about the economics just yet," Bo says. "But we lean toward a more socialist approach in our community."

I mull over the information. "That's larger than I expected. Rhode Island is only, what, 1,500 square miles?"

I can see the pride in Bo's face when he talks about his community. "We like to have space to stretch our legs. Our people don't do well in tight areas. If you come to stay with us, you'll see that most of our people live in single-family homes. Our city doesn't look like your typical urban city, more like a suburb. We don't really do apartment buildings or condos. You won't see high-rises packed full of people. There are some office-type buildings that stand out, but even they have a 5-story height restriction."

"What about the culture?" I ask. "Is there diversity in religion? Is there a class structure? How is the education system?"

Bo pinches his eyebrows together in thought as he says, "No, yes, equivalent to undergraduate."

His vague answer must mean that the secret lies somewhere in their culture. He says that there isn't any religious diversity. What type of religion requires above-top-secret concealment?

"What about doctors, architects, and engineers?" I ask. "How do they obtain their education?"

With a laugh, Bo says, "Ellie, my people aren't locked up in some cult-like commune. Many of our people leave to pursue advanced degrees in everything from healthcare to art history. Most come back to our community, some decide to explore the world. It isn't that different from a normal city in the United States."

I lean in closer and say in a conspiratorial tone, "But normal cities let new people move in, and I'm guessing that you don't."

There goes that slight head tilt of his again. "You're only partially right. I can't elaborate on our immigration policy, but there is a policy, and newcomers must meet certain requirements."

I am finding this community more and more intriguing by the minute.

Checking his phone, Bo sees a message and types a short response.

"My advisors are eager to meet you," he says. "Why don't we head to my hotel, and we can all have lunch in my suite. It'll give us some privacy to talk, and you can get to know my crew."

Chapter Four

I am not surprised when we enter one of the most expensive hotels in D.C. I wonder if Bo, his community, or the U.S. taxpayers are paying for the elaborate space. I guess it's better to spend taxpayer money on a room for an *actual* foreign leader than a high-priced mistress with a fake title, which happens more often than I would like to think about.

I take the opportunity to ask about it in the penthouse elevator. "This is a pretty fancy hotel," I say. "Did we pick it or did you?"

Bo smirks at me for a moment before he answers. "Still trying to work out that economic information, huh?"

I only shrug in response.

"I paid for this hotel from my own pocket," Bo says. "I'm certainly not the richest man in this town, but I do OK. I like this hotel because there is a good amount of privacy."

Bo holds the door to his private suite open for me, and as I walk past him, I see a woman standing with her back toward us.

I am immediately struck by her long, thick, dark brown hair. It's in a simple braid down her back and reaches all the way to her butt. It's the thickest braid I have ever seen, and I wonder if she has extensions in her hair to make it that long and thick.

I watch her turn, and when she sees me, she smiles warmly. Suddenly, I realize that I never asked Bo if he is married or has a family. I have no idea if this is his wife, an assistant, or a member of his council. Hell, she could be the cleaning lady for all I know.

As she gets closer to us, I can see that she looks older than Bo and me, maybe in her mid-40s or early 50s. Her build is slim but not skinny. She is wearing a T-shirt and light-colored skinny jeans with casual slip-on shoes. I can see the muscle definition in her arms.

They are toned but not bulky, similar to my own. As she walks, I can't help but notice how she moves with a level of grace that makes me think of a gymnast or dancer. When she comes to stand near me, we are nearly identical in height.

Her face has an exotic look, with high cheekbones and almond-shaped eyes. Her skin is tan, and I wonder if she is of Middle Eastern descent.

"You must be Eloise," she says. Her tone and overall demeanor are warm, like she is going to turn around with a plate of fresh cookies at any moment. I instantly like her. "I'm Candance Baker, one of Bo's advisors. Everyone calls me Candy. Yes, my name is Candy Baker, no, I don't actually make candy. Yes, my parents thought it was hysterical."

I let out a small snort as I try not to outright laugh. "You must give that speech a lot. You should get that printed on a business card or something. Please, call me Ellie. I am very glad to meet you."

Bo playfully scolds Candy for being so impatient to meet me.

"I couldn't help myself," she replies. "When Bo told us that he found an ambassador who he thought might fit into our community, I just about fainted. Bo is very protective of us. After we spent so much time talking about you and your work, I just couldn't wait another moment to meet you."

Bo rolls his eyes at Candy and shakes his head. There is a knock at the door, and Bo walks over to open it for his remaining council members.

Both are men. The first, Chester Frekison, has a very California surfer-dude vibe. I would guess he is about 30, which surprises me. He has striking blue eyes and light hair that is a little too long on top to look totally professional, but not so long that it's sloppy. He has a slimmer build than Bo, but he is also clearly athletic.

The second, Roman Bernulf, is older, maybe in his 60s. He has a thick head of dark brown hair with some gray and white showing through around the temples. His close-cropped beard reveals two patches of white hair, one on either side of his chin. For a man of his age, he looks to be in great shape. He is the definition of burly, and I can almost imagine him in a striped leotard holding an oversized dumbbell at a carnival.

One thing is for sure: this secret sovereign nation community likes to stay in shape. I am suddenly very thankful for my toned build. Normally, when I enter a new community, I like to adopt their fashion. Looking like everyone else helps you fit in with everyone else, which makes people more comfortable around you, which leads to trust. I have a feeling that it will be my body type that helps me assimilate into this community.

If I do decide to accept the job, I will just need to keep up my intense workout routine.

When our room service arrives, we all take a seat in the small dining area. Candy and Bo hand out plates of food to each of us.

"I think we'll have plenty of time for work over the next few days, so why don't we take this time to get to know each other better?" Bo says to the group of us. "Ellie, why don't you start by telling us more about you? What's your favorite sport? Do you have any hobbies? Hidden talents? And most importantly, do you prefer cats or dogs?"

I can't help but laugh. This feels less like a job interview and more like meeting a boyfriend's parents. Bo and his advisors have an easy way about them. They are clearly very close, and they really do look more like a family than a political council. It's not common amongst established governments to have this type of commodore, there is always some type of tension or rivalry between high-ranking politicians.

"OK," I say. "I'll go first. I don't follow any professional sports. I moved around too much to ever get invested in a single team. I do like to play soccer, but I'm not really good at it. I spend my free time doing a lot of yoga. It forces me to release the stress of whatever project I am working on. As for hidden talent, well, it's sort of weird, but I have an encyclopedic knowledge of surname origins and meanings that I've picked up through the years from living in different countries all over the world. And lastly, I love all animals, but I'll have to go with dogs."

Roman looks at me with wide eyes, "Surnames, huh? Then let's hear it, young lady. What can you tell us about our origins?"

I start with Bernulf, which is old German and means like a bear. I find it a fitting name for the giant man. Next is Frekison, which I surmise is Swedish and related to the wolf of Odin, though I haven't actually encountered the name before and can only guess. Next is Baker, which is old English and, not surprisingly, means to dry with heat or bake. Lastly, we get to Ragnulf, Nordic and roughly means warrior wolf.

The table is quiet, and all eyes are on me. As I look from one person to the next, I don't detect any offense, it is more like bewilderment.

"I told you it was a weird talent," I say with a shrug and take my seat.

The group continues the conversation, taking turns telling me a little bit about themselves as they go. They can't say too much, apparently. So, I am left with only surface knowledge about each person.

What I do learn, is that these folks eat. I have never seen so much food disappear so quickly. Also, they do not share food easily. I swear I heard someone growl.

※

The week flies by. Bo and I fall into a rhythm pretty quickly. Morning coffee with the crew, followed by budget requests, civil engineering, census status reviews, and city event planning. All of it mundane and normal governmental chores.

By the time we wrap up the council meeting on Friday afternoon, I have learned a lot about Bo's city-nation while also learning nothing about it. I know there are open storefronts in the city center that Candy wants to incentivize. I know the in-community postal service is being bogged down by all the online ordering from inside the community, and Chester thinks that there is enough consistent strain to warrant a new truck and driver position. I know that there is a potential wash-out along a back road heading out to several large homesteads that Roman thinks should be bumped up the list of civil engineering projects.

I know that they face many of the same problems as all metropolitan areas. School district lines need to be reviewed since some schools are overcrowded, and others are half-empty. Power consumption is up, and they aren't sure if the current grid can sustain the growth. The list goes on and on.

While all these issues are important for the community, they are common for any government and don't require the services of a dedicated U.S. Ambassador. State-level representatives handle these issues all day long throughout the United States.

None of these issues gives me any clues as to why I am here.

Bo and I say goodbye to Candy, Roman, and Chester. Since it is our last day meeting before I must make my final decision, I hug each of them, unsure if I will ever see them again. They are all flying back to their homes tomorrow, and unless I agree to the position and the Secretary of State and Bo accept me, I won't even know where home is for them.

Bo closes the door behind him and takes a seat in the chair opposite of me. "You're scowling," he says. "Tell me what you're thinking."

I take a deep cleansing breath to organize my thoughts before I even attempt to explain to Bo what's on my mind. After a week with him and the advisory council, I know a lot about the "normal" workings of his community. But none of that helps me understand what this job is about. I have no idea what will be expected of me because I have no idea what makes this community so special. Whatever it is that makes Bo and his people "not normal" is exactly what I need to know to do my job. But I can't know what the job is until I have already accepted the job.

"First, I don't scowl," I say with a playful grin. "Second, I'm just contemplating. I am about to make the biggest decision of my life, and I only have information that doesn't really matter for that decision. Does that make sense?"

Bo leans back in his chair and nods. His normally playful eyes take on a more serious look.

"I know it's hard, Ellie, you don't want to commit to a job that you don't really know anything about. But I disagree that the information you have is irrelevant to your decision. What you have already learned about my advisors and my people is very relevant."

Bo takes a deep breath, and I give him the space to formulate his words.

"What you have learned this week might not give away our big secret, but it shows you who we are as people, who it is that you will be working to protect. It was important to me that you learned about us as a people before you started looking at us as a top secret program. I need to protect my people, above everything else. That means making sure that our liaison values them as real-life, living, breathing people with families, jobs, pets, hopes, and dreams. They have meaning and value beyond what they can do for your government. I can't make the decision for you, but I can tell you that I truly believe that you are the right person for the job. I wouldn't have invested the time and effort to come out here, travel my advisors out here, and camp out in this horrendously overpopulated city if I didn't know for certain that you could handle the truth."

"You did say that your people like to spread out," I say with a forced smile.

"We do," he says with a smile. "I can't wait to get back to my ranch, smell the fresh air, and listen to the quiet. This place is noisy 24/7, and it smells awful all the time. I don't know why anyone would live here."

"It's not my favorite place in the world either," I say. "But honestly, it's the closest I have to a hometown. We always came back here between assignments. I spent more time here than in any other city. What if I'm not built to stay in one place?"

Bo looks at me with a seriousness that turns his good-looking face into that of a strikingly handsome man. I realize that I haven't been looking at him as a president, or king, or whatever his title is. Until this moment, I have regarded him as though we were equals. His casual demeanor over the last week has put me so at ease that I forgot that he is a powerful man, and ultimately, could hold my fate in the palm of his hands.

"I think that you are built to help people," Bo says in a tone that leaves no room for argument. "I don't think the location matters, I think the work matters. Besides, just because you'll have a home base, doesn't mean you won't still be traveling."

Another piece of the puzzle falls into place. Are more of these secret communities out there? How many are there? Are they in the U.S.? Do other countries know about them?

Every bit of information I glean just adds to the list of questions.

"Look," Bo continues as I start gathering my things to leave for the weekend. "I know that I am asking you to take a lot on faith here. I am asking you to trust me because I know that you're the one."

Chapter Five

I sit in my short-term rental apartment and look around at the bare walls and my meager belongings. It's 5 a.m. Monday morning, and I am once again preparing to meet with Secretary of State Viktor.

Only this time, I know why I am going there.

Not that it helps me any. I spent the entire weekend writing and re-writing "Pros and Cons" lists to try to help me make the right decision.

Pros:
1. Bo seems like a genuinely great guy
2. He's easy to look at
3. Candy, Chester, and Roman are all really nice
4. Knowledge of top secret stuff
5. Help keep a community safe
6. Get away from Morris and Larry

Cons:
1. No idea what the secret is
2. No idea where I will be living
3. No idea what my job will entail
4. Can't ever tell anyone about my job
5. Settling down into a home base forever
6. Fear of the unknown is a real thing

Turns out that I'm no help to myself. I wish my parents were here. If I could just talk it through with them, they would know what to do. They had the same drive that I do to help make the world a little bit better. They wouldn't think twice about the fact that no one can know what I am doing, because it was never about recognition, it was about doing good for the sake of doing good.

On the other hand, if they were here, I might not even have been considered for this assignment. Seems like my lack of attachments was part of the reason they came to me.

What would they say? Probably something along the lines of "helping people is the most important thing we can do in this life, Ellie." Or "What does your heart say?" Or "If not you, then who?"

Ugh, it doesn't take Freud to figure out that my subconscious has already decided that I should take the job. I know from our talk on Friday that Bo thinks I am right for the position, and he has all the facts at his disposal. He thinks that I can handle it. No, actually, he *believes* I can, which is even stronger.

The problem is that I am putting my future in the hands of a man I have only known for a week. Granted, I think that I am a pretty good judge of character. Bo seems very genuine, and his advisors have shown that they have great admiration and respect for him.

Even if I don't trust his motives towards me, I have to believe that he wouldn't put his people at risk by putting me in a position to fail.

Besides, what could he possibly gain by setting me up for failure? I'm essentially a nobody in the political arena. I don't come from money. I don't have ties to anyone of influence.

Let's be totally honest, can I really live the rest of my life *not knowing* the secret?

At 7 a.m. I head out the door to make my way to the Secretary of State's office. Looks like I am going to sign my life away, quite literally.

※

"I have to say, Ms. Margrave," Secretary Viktor says. "I am very pleased to hear that you will be accepting the assignment. Bo tells me that you two get on well and that his council members are all in agreement that you are the right person for the job."

"Ellie has made quiet the impression on my team, Allan," Bo says, casually dropping the Secretary's first name like we are all besties.

"Thank you, Secretary Viktor, Mr. Ragnulf," I say. I am still wildly anxious about this next step in my life, but there's no going back now.

We spend the next couple of hours filling out paperwork and making sure that all my credentials are in order. I'm issued a laptop, tablet, and cell phone for secure communications with the Secretary of State's office and anyone else that I may need to contact securely.

We review protocols and cover stories.

I'm issued credentials for the FBI, for any interactions relating to local police forces, whatever that means. I am briefed on protocols and procedures for intercepting any of Bo's people who might have been arrested or are being detained by police.

I am also issued credentials for Homeland Security in case of any media coverage that needs to be repressed. This is another oddity to explore later.

My new heavily encrypted laptop contains file after file of training material on handling any situation that may attract unwanted attention to the Ulfserkir people.

Bo's people are called Ulfserkir. I'll have to ask him about it, but it seems Nordic, maybe wolf warrior or fighter. I guess it makes sense that their leader would be named Warrior Wolf.

Turning my attention back to the Secretary and Bo, I realize that we are being dismissed from the office. "Ms. Margrave," Secretary Viktor says. "Again, congratulations on your new assignment. My office will handle all of the backend paperwork with Morris. You are free to go ahead with Bo and start getting settled into your new role."

Slightly stunned, I closed the lid on my new laptop and shake the Secretary's hand before stuffing everything into the very nice leather laptop bag that the tech guys brought me.

"Thank you, sir," I say, and Bo and I both leave the office.

Walking out to the street, I try to pace my steps and calm my breathing. I can feel my adrenaline kicking up. I need to calm myself down. I can't have a panic attack on my first day as an ambassador to these Nordic wolf-fighting people, or whoever they are.

I start giving myself an internal pep talk. Pull it together, Ellie. You'll be fine. Everything is fine. This is totally fine.

Thankfully, just as I'm starting to falter and believe that maybe this isn't fine, Bo leans in and whispers, "Let's drop off your bag in my room and get a drink."

"A drink? Are you insane?" I'm so stunned that I stop walking for a moment. Catching up to him, I add, "We can't go to a bar right now. One, it's only 11 a.m. And two, I need you to read me in, I've got to know the big secret."

"Ellie," he says as calmly as ever, hands in his pockets, and steps an effortless glide. "Relax. We can talk in the bar about a lot of this. There probably won't be anyone in there at this time of day. Trust me, it's a lot to cover, and it's best to start slow and build a picture of who we are. There is a *lot* you don't understand yet, and you are definitely going to want to have a drink or two in you for this part."

Reluctantly, I follow him to the hotel and do exactly as he's suggested. I leave my new laptop, tablet, and phone in the room and head with him down to the hotel bar. As predicted, we are the only people here.

Bo orders a beer and gets me a vodka and cranberry. I'm not sure if we look like raging alcoholics or nervous adulterers, but the bartender doesn't seem to care either way. My guess is that he probably sees a lot of both in D.C.

Bo leads me to a table in the back corner, well away from the bar. We are essentially alone and able to talk openly here.

"OK," I say to him as we sit, "spill it."

Laughing, Bo takes a slow sip of his beer. "Let's start with the easy stuff. We're a closed community with our capital in Oregon, with a small part of our land crossing into Washington state. That is the main community. But we have smaller communities throughout the U.S. and Canada. I rule over all of those communities. We are not the only community of our type. There are others in Germany, Iceland, Africa, and Asia. I do *not* rule over those communities, but we do have close relationships with them, and we all fall under the same main leader. All of us are connected through our shared genetics, and we obey the same basic laws."

I listen intently to what he is saying, but I stop him here. "What do you mean by shared genetics? Are you all related?"

"No," Bo continues. "Not the way you're thinking. We are linked by common ancestors. Everyone in my community and everyone like us around the world are all descendants of an ancient race. We all share similar DNA that is very different from your DNA. But we are getting ahead of ourselves."

I'm already completely confused by what I am hearing. Honestly, it doesn't make much sense. What's the big deal about a genetic anomaly or some sort of common ancestry? Why would that constitute a top secret declaration? My head is already spinning, and we haven't even gotten to anything good yet.

At least one thing is for sure, Bo was right, I'm glad I have a drink for this. "OK, so you are all related, but not actual cousins. Got it."

"And here I thought it would be hard to explain," Bo laughs and motions to my almost empty glass. "Do you want another drink before I continue?"

Considering that I've just been told that I work for comic book mutants, I nod, and Bo gets up and walks to the bar for another beer and vodka cranberry. I watch him carefully as he moves through the space. Aside from his above-average size and athletic grace, there isn't anything unusual about him. What could this genetic difference be? Why is it such a big secret?

"Here you go," he says, setting my new drink down in front of me. "So, what else can I answer now? You asked me last week about the culture of my people and about our economics. As a rule, we believe in community first, so when a new family comes to us, either created through marriage or they relocate to our lands, we provide that family with a home and food. We arrange employment and we make sure that they find a place in our community. We don't tax our people, and we don't require them to purchase the land that they live on. We believe in sharing our resources. Successes and losses are spread equally. We do use American money, and all workers are paid. The difference is that, without needing to spend most of their income on basic necessities, our people are free to spend their money on life. We can also pay our employees much less per hour, which makes our profit margins on any exported product much higher. That profit is then put right back into the community. We use that money to fund our schools, infrastructure, and social programs."

Now it's my turn to tilt my head in surprise. "That's amazing," I say with genuine wonder. "Can you really support every member of the community? You have no poverty, hunger, or homelessness?"

I can see the genuine pride in Bo's face when he talks about his community. He isn't boasting about his personal accomplishments as much as he is sharing the joy and love he has for his home.

"That's right," he says. "We live as a pack. We take care of each other because our community is only as strong as our weakest members. Since everyone looks out for each other and everyone has a stake in the success of each family and every business within our community, we have very little crime. Our families raise their kids together and help each other whenever they can. It's a point of pride for one of us to help another pack member who needs it. Lifting up one family lifts up the entire community."

I finish my second drink in a large gulp, but I decline a third. I need to keep a clear head. Things are already getting a little strange.

While we were talking, the bar started to fill with the lunchtime crowd. Bo and I decide that it would be better to take this discussion upstairs.

"I have so many questions," I say as we get into the elevator.

After we walk into Bo's suite, he offers to order us lunch. I agree. We'll probably be here for a while, and I have a belly full of booze right now.

After making the call for some food, Bo returns to the sitting area and takes the chair across from me.

"What can I answer for you now?" Bo asks when I finally look up at him.

"The packet I got from Secretary Victor has a lot of information about keeping your people out of trouble with local authorities," I say. "What's the deal with that?"

Bo takes a breath and runs his fingers through his hair. This question is making him uncomfortable for some reason. Interesting.

"Until you know the whole story," he says, "some of this won't make sense. I am going to need you to take some things on faith for right now. I promise you that I will explain everything, but a lot of the information that we need to cover is going to seem crazy when taken without context. I need you to trust me, and if you can't do that, at least trust your Secretary of State."

At his words, I can feel a tension creeping into my body. Before responding, I take a deep breath and lean forward a little. "OK," I say. "I'll try my best to trust your process and let you tell your story in the way that you need to tell it."

Chapter Six

After a long pause, Bo seems to have his thoughts together enough to speak again. "We need to keep my people out of police custody to keep our blood and DNA out of your labs. We also need to keep my people out of your prisons, because our kind must be allowed certain freedoms that a normal human prison doesn't allow for. If we aren't granted these freedoms, the results could be catastrophic for any normal human in our vicinity."

Bo is right, this sounds crazy. What does he mean by "normal human" prison? How far does this difference in DNA go? *Catastrophic*, what? What did I get myself involved with? Are these really some kind of mutants, lepers maybe? What is going on?

I must be making a weird face because Bo pauses and shifts in his chair. He takes a deep breath and decides to stand instead. It's weird to see him so unnerved. Since meeting him, I have come to expect unwavering confidence and an almost annoying air of ease and comfort.

His discomfort does nothing to ease my rapid heart rate and raging anxiety.

"OK," he says while starting to pace back and forth in front of his chair. "To understand who we are, you must first understand that there are things out there that humans are just oblivious to. There are other species of beings that exist, and humans are, for the most part, completely ignorant of them."

I raise my eyebrows and ask, "So, like, aliens?"

"In a manner of speaking," Bo says. "When you think of aliens, you usually think of little guys in spaceships. But what if, instead of spaceships, they used wormholes to travel between planets?"

"I know I said that I would let you tell your story," I say with a slight pitch to my voice. I'm trying hard to stay calm and have an open mind, but honestly, I am starting to freak out a little. "With all due respect, what the fuck are we talking about right now? Are you telling me that your people are from outer space? That you're aliens?"

Bo rubs his face with both hands, "This isn't going exactly the way I had hoped. No, I'm not saying that we are from outer space, exactly."

He pauses, and I can almost see him physically collecting his thoughts. As he is about to continue, the food arrives, and we have to stop to let the waiter in. Bo asks him to just leave the cart and ushers him out of the room as quickly as possible.

Once he is gone, Bo arranges the food and drinks on the small coffee table in front of me and hands me a plate. As I toy with my food, I start taking a critical look at Bo. He's bigger than most men, very symmetrical, annoyingly handsome with great bone structure.

He moves with a grace that I wouldn't expect from a man his size. I wonder if he ever took ballet, that's something football players do, right? I'm pretty sure I read that somewhere.

Taking his seat in front of me again, Bo continues. "Keep in mind that everything I am about to tell you is easily provable. And I will show you as soon as you are ready. I think I'm just going to rip the bandage and lay it out."

Bo stands and starts pacing again while muttering under his breath. I get the very distinct impression that this is the first time that he has given this talk. I am the first Ambassador, right? Who told the other government officials about the alien/leper/mutant people if it wasn't Bo?

My mind is starting to race again, so I take a couple of deep breaths and a bite of some sort of roll that came with my salad. While I try to calm my own mind, I watch Bo pace back and forth collecting his own thoughts. I have to consciously stop myself from rushing him. Didn't he say he was going to rip the bandage off? Does that mean something else where he is from?

Finally, after what must have been 5 full minutes, Bo stops pacing and turns to face me.

"Remember when you said that you like dogs?" he asks.

Of all the things that I was preparing myself to hear, that was not on the list. I am confused again. This is completely out of left field. I decide to just ride this wave and see where the hell he is going with this. "Yeah, I like dogs."

Bo stops pacing and turns to face me. He raises his palms in an "I surrender" gesture. Is he trying to look non-threatening?

"Well, that's great, because my people, we can turn into wolves," he says. "We are what you would call werewolves. Not like your movies and books, but I can explain more about that later. We turn into what looks like a regular, but abnormally large wolf. It's more in line with what the Native Americans called Skinwalkers or shapeshifters. We can change at will, not just during a full moon. I guess we'll talk about that more later, too."

I jump to my feet, hold up my hands, and shake my head at him all at once. "Whoa, whoa, stop," I say a little too loudly. "You are telling me that you are freaking werewolves from space?"

"Shit," Bo says, sitting back down in his chair and running his hand through his hair again. "No, not space. I got a little off track with that. But the idea of traveling through a wormhole is relevant to how we came to be here. I can tell you the whole story about our lineage and how we evolved from the werewolves of myth to the very human-looking people we are today."

I drop my hands to my sides with a thud. "Great, I can't wait," I say a little too sharply. In my defense, this is absolutely insane. Of all the things that I thought Bo was going to say, this was nowhere near even my wildest ideas. I did *not* have shapeshifter wolf on my bingo card.

Did the Secretary of State lose a bet to Morris, and this is all an elaborate prank? Is that possible? I mean, it would be crazy, but not as crazy as werewolf aliens from wormholes. This has to be some sort of punishment, right? Maybe good ol' Larry has something on the SoS, too? Oh my god, was I drugged at the bar? Is this a hallucination?

I sit back in my chair and gesture for Bo to continue. If this is some sort of sick prank or drug-induced fever dream, it's best to get it all over with—the sooner, the better.

"I'll start with the wormholes. We call them portals, and they don't go to another point within your idea of space. Instead, they allow beings to cross from one dimension to another. There are several different dimensions and portals that can take you from one dimension to another. Right now, let's just focus on the dimension, or realm, that your ancestors called Ulfheðnar, as in wolf skinwalker. That's where my ancestors come from. They are known in your history as Berserkers. They don't look like me. They walk upright, but they still look a lot like a wolf. They are covered in hair and have elongated faces. They can shift into a very large wolf when they care to, but in that form, they aren't capable of speech. So, they spend most of their time upright. They are definitely the inspiration for the werewolf of legend. The half-man/half-wolf creature roaming the woods looking for unsuspecting teenagers. Except, that is how they look all the time."

Bo pauses to take a few bites of food and a sip of water while I absorb everything he has just said.

"I guess that explains the Nordic names," I say, trying to lighten the atmosphere. If this is some giant prank, I won't give them the satisfaction of watching me freak out.

"You know," Bo says with a smirk, "That name thing you did, it had us all a little worried. We thought you had figured us out."

I actually snort. "Are you kidding? What kind of sane person thinks to themselves, these people have animal-themed names, they must be werewolves. That's not a normal thought at all."

I take another bite of my chicken and mindlessly chew it without really tasting it. I start running through all that Bo has told me so far.

"Can I ask you something?" I say.

Bo nods while he chews a bite of his steak.

"You keep referring to these, how do you say that...Olf-heth-nar...creatures in the present tense. Are you telling me that they still exist?"

Bo nods. "Oh yeah, there is a whole dimension of them. They just don't come here a lot anymore. Time moves differently across the dimensions. Most are close to each other, but the Ulfheðnar dimension moves much slower than this one. The story goes that, after a mighty battle alongside their Viking comrades, the Ulfheðnar returned to their dimension to honor their dead. While they believed that they had been gone for only a year or two, generations had gone by in this realm. When they sought out their Viking friends, they found new cities and new people, and no one remembered them. Instead, people hunted them as monsters. Sad and angry, they returned to their home realm and labeled this realm and all the humans living here as unworthy of their friendship."

I mull over what he is saying. "So, the legends of the Berserkers, the men who wore animal skins and fought like monsters, they were actually the Olf-heth-nar? It makes sense, I guess. Your grandfather tells you a story of how he fought next to the wolfmen warriors. Over time, having not seen any actual wolfmen, the story changes to men dressed as wolves. But that doesn't explain you. How do we get from living legend werewolves to modern-day wolf men and women?"

Bo nods. "We are the descendants of the women who were taken as trophies from the villages conquered by the Vikings and Ulfheðnar. You are familiar with the unfortunate way that those women were treated. Many of those women bore children who were half-human, half-wolfman. A lot of those women and children died, but for the ones who lived, their human DNA and Ulfheðnar DNA found a way to co-exist. For the most part, we look human. We are stronger, we have keener senses, and most notably, we can turn into wolves."

I lean away from my food and take a sip of my water. As wild as this story is, it makes a strange sort of sense. If this is a prank, Larry must have hired one hell of an actor and screenwriter.

"Why keep the secret?" I ask.

"You of all people know how the world really is," Bo says a bit somberly. "We have tried to co-exist in the open, and it has never worked out. We were hunted and slaughtered in droves by humans throughout history. The Spanish Inquisition and Salem Witch Trials are just a couple of examples of the persecution of innocent non-humans. Men fear what they don't know, or don't understand. They fear anything that is different. And that fear is very dangerous."

I do understand how the world is, and Bo isn't wrong. I think back to my primary school education and how the teachers told us that the villagers in Salem were controlled by fear. In college, we learned that the murders were likely politically motivated. Men controlling their town with fear, covering up abuses and affairs.

It was the same with the Inquisition. The corrupted Church leaders killed any who opposed them. All in a bid for power.

Could they have actually been killing those who were different from them? Beings who they believed were a threat?

"I'll be honest with you, Bo. This makes a compelling story, but you said you have proof for me when I'm ready. I don't think I can entertain any more of this without some kind of proof. A large part of me thinks that someone is going to jump out of the closet with a camera and yell 'gotcha' at me any moment."

Bo smiles widely and stands from the table.

"I'll be right back; I just have to grab a blanket and get out of these jeans."

Chapter Seven

When Bo finally returns to the sitting area, he is shirtless and has a blanket wrapped around his waist.

My jaw literally drops open at the sight. Not because he has an amazing body, which he absolutely does, but because this is completely insane.

"What the hell are you doing?" I say. Complete shock causing me to jump from my chair. Reflexively, I start putting distance between myself and the probably naked man in front of me.

"It's not what you think," Bo says, raising his hand and almost losing his grip on the blanket.

"HEY," I yell. "Both hands on the blanket, buddy."

Bo laughs, he actually laughs. This isn't funny. I am in a hotel room, alone, with the leader of a secret sovereign nation, and he is butt-ass naked. He's also, quite possibly, full-on-level-5-crazy-pants.

"I'm sorry," Bo says when he sees some of the anger and fear in my expression. "I just really like those jeans, and if I shift in them, they'll be ruined."

I cover my face with both hands. Taking a few calming breaths, I face Bo again.

"What are you talking about?" I say as calmly as I can. If he is, in fact, a lunatic, I don't want to upset him.

"I told you that I could prove that what I was saying is true," Bo says calmly. "What better way than to show you? Seeing is believing, right?"

"OK," I say. "So, what, you're just going to transform into a giant wolf?"

Bo looks a little unsure of his plan now.

"Yes, but you have to promise that you won't run out of here screaming. I can't chase you out of here in wolf form, and when I shift back, I'll be naked. That's probably worse than chasing you as a wolf. Also, I will be able to hear and understand all that you say, but I can't talk back to you. You can ask me to come closer or move back, and I will do it. When you are ready, I'll shift back into my human form, ok?"

I throw my hands up, exasperated. This is by far the craziest thing that I have ever heard.

"OK, fine, let's do this," I say. This is why I stay single. All the hot ones are bat-shit crazy. They seem so normal at first, then, bam, they hit you full force with the crazy train.

"I am going to go very quickly, and you won't be able to see much of the process. It can look a bit gruesome in slow motion, and I am not sure you want to see that."

With that, Bo starts to bend in half, and before my eyes…hair, and paws, and a freaking tail.

"Fucking shit!" I yell involuntarily. I instinctively jump back, smacking into the dining table.

The wolf Bo lets out a whine and backs up. It tilts its chestnut brown head to the side…holy fuck…it's just like Bo. I mean, it is Bo, right? This must be what a psychotic break feels like. This can't be real. Men don't turn into giant fucking dogs.

OK, I have to pull myself together. It can understand me, right?

"Bo," I ask. "If that's really you in there, put up your right hand…foot…paw…whatever."

The fucking wolf-dog-man looks at me and I swear it is smiling when it holds up its right leg, paw in the air like it's waiting for a fucking high-five.

"This can't be real," I say to more myself than to the wolf thing. He starts to take a step toward me and hold up my hands. "Whoa there, back up."

He puts his ears down like a scolded puppy and steps backward.

This is too much.

"Bring back Bo," I say in a half yell. I am starting to panic, and I can feel adrenaline flooding my body. I need to sit.

Before I can even get to the chair, my vision goes blurry. Darkness is creeping in. I'm going to pass out, and there is nothing I can do to stop it.

※

When I open my eyes, I see a very human-looking Bo face staring back at me. I feel around and realize that I am on the couch.

Bo is kneeling on the floor to my right.

"What happened?" I ask.

"You fainted. Probably from shock." Bo says.

Turning my head toward him, I see his bare chest. I quickly turn to face the back of the couch. "Please tell me that you aren't naked right now."

"I have my blanket," Bo says softly.

I refuse to confirm his story by looking. When I try to sit up, he puts his hand on the back of my shoulder to guide me.

"Let me get you some water," he says. "Don't try to stand yet."

I let him hand me the water before I say, "Can you please put your clothes back on now?"

He doesn't say anything more. He just stands and walks to the bedroom.

When Bo returns, I have gathered my thoughts, and I feel a little less foggy. I remember him turning into a wolf, and then I remember that I demanded he turn back into himself. That's when I fainted.

I guess it isn't surprising that I would pass out from shock. At least I managed to keep my promise, and I didn't run out of the hotel screaming. This can't be real, right? Men don't turn into wolves. Right?

"So, you are all like this," I ask. "Even Candy?"

Bo smiles. "Yes, even Candy."

"The Secretary of State knows about this," I say with a bit of skepticism. "Has he personally witnessed you turn into a giant wolf?"

Bo sits next to me on the couch. I think he's afraid that I'll pass out again.

"Yes. Secretary Viktor knows about us. What we are and what we can do," Bo says. "But, no, he's never seen it in person. He was briefed about us when he took office and shown a series of military videos showing soldiers changing into wolves to escape capture or sneak up on enemies."

Bo runs a hand through his hair before continuing.

"It's part of our deal with your government. We allow some of our men to enlist in the military, strictly top secret missions. We can sneak in and out in our wolf forms. In exchange, we live here unbothered by the government. We have access to U.S. passports and can travel the world like any normal citizen."

I nod as he speaks. It all makes sense. I guess a few wolf-men who were trained as assassins could do more than an entire platoon of soldiers. They could slip in and out, unseen and unheard. No one could pin the crime on our government.

"The CIA must love you guys," I say. "But what am I here for? You already have the backing of the highest-ranking officials in every branch of law enforcement and the White House. What the hell am I doing here?"

"I can't call the director of the FBI every time one of my people gets into a bar fight and is arrested for assault," Bo says, turning his body on the couch to face me more. "We have been trying to handle things in-house as much as possible. But with camera phones and security cameras everywhere, it is getting harder and harder to keep our secrets. Secretary Viktor thought that a dedicated liaison to the outside world could ease the stress on us, and the U.S. government, by handling the local police and local government officials. Every few years, some local Rep or new Governor will come along and demand that we start paying property taxes. Or try to take our land through some bullshit lawsuit. Occasionally, our truck drivers will get pulled over and detained by local police who think we are human traffickers or drug runners. Humans still fear anyone who is different. And we need you to help us bridge that gap. We need you to help us keep our people out of your prisons and keep our blood out of your labs."

"What happens if one of you is sent to a human prison?" I ask.

"At first," Bo says, "nothing. But if we don't shift into our wolf form voluntarily, after a few months, we *will* shift whether we like it or not. When we repress that side of us for too long, it can become manic. It's hard to explain. When I shift into a wolf, I am physically and emotionally a wolf, but I am also still me. It takes practice to bring your human logic to the front of the wolf's mind so that you can override the wolf's instincts when you need to. It is difficult for me to explain it because I have never been human, so I don't fully understand what it's like to only have one side of yourself. Just like you can't understand what it is like for us to be two beings with one brain. When I am in my human form, I am still a wolf; I just use more human logic than wolf instinct. It's almost like our brain flips when we shift. It is the same consciousness, but a different part of the brain is in charge. When one of us tries to suppress our wolf personality for extended periods of time, we can become mentally fractured. Then, when the wolf does come out, we will be all instinct and rage. It takes hours, sometimes days, before a manic wolf will calm down enough to allow its human logic to resurface. By then, it's usually carnage."

I take a deep breath, and then another. All of this is so unbelievable, but I saw it. I watched a man turn into a wolf right in front of me. I looked into its eyes and saw the man inside the wolf.

I talked to it for God's sake.

"What do you do with the prisoners?" I ask. "I get that they can't stay in a human jail, but if they committed a crime, they need to be held accountable."

Bo nods his head in agreement. "We have our own detention center. We also conduct our own investigations before we put any of our people in jail. Most of the time, the issue that gets them in trouble is related to their being a wolf. I can't tell you where I was if I was out for a wolf run. I can't explain how my innocent shove sent a drunk guy halfway through a wall. A lot of times, when we refuse to talk to the police, or they can't find any information on us, they arrest us for obstruction. Or worse, they do find out that we are Ulfserkir, and they arrest us on suspicion of being different."

I know enough about the world, and bigots in general, to believe that. According to Bo, his community is 800,000, but there are others around the world. Potentially millions of werewolves are living and working alongside humans every single day.

"Are there any wolves in the government?" I ask.

"No," Bo says. "We aren't interested in your politics or power struggles. It has been the great fallacy of humans to believe that just because we are stronger than you, that means we want to rule you. I see the men in power in your world. Any 16-year-old human girl could probably beat most of them in a fistfight. The thirst for control over your fellow man has nothing to do with physical strength."

I don't know what to say to that, so I just nod my head.

"You know what," Bo says. "It's been a really long day for you. Why don't we call it a day, and we can talk again tomorrow?"

I nod. "I think that is an excellent idea. This has been a lot, to say the least."

Chapter Eight

Surprisingly, I sleep like a log.

The constantly racing thoughts left me completely exhausted, and I was asleep as soon as I hit my bed. I didn't even dream, at least not that I can remember.

The next morning, while my coffee is brewing, I turn on my new work cell phone. A few numbers are already programmed in there. I text Bo from the new phone, asking him when and where we should meet today.

There is still so much I don't understand. A million questions I need to answer.

Not to mention, I need to set a time frame for moving to Oregon.

I'll have to make a point to discuss my start date and the move details with Bo first thing. I don't want to get off track and let another day slide by without nailing down my time frame and living arrangements.

Not that I need much time to pack my things. A lifetime of nomadic living has trained me to live a bare-bones lifestyle. I have perfected my closet with enough mix-and-match clothing pieces that I can give the illusion of a large wardrobe. You'd be surprised what you can do with jewelry and some fancy belts.

I don't have knick-knacks or houseplants. Aside from the few photo albums that I keep with photos of my parents and myself through the years, I don't have anything personal in my entire apartment.

I can pack the whole place up and be ready to leave in under an hour. I don't own the furniture, the artwork on the walls, or the dishes in the kitchen—they all came with the rental.

Even the linens are rented.

Just another reason that I was perfect for this assignment. I can disappear from here today, and no one would be the wiser. How many people can move away without telling anyone where they are going and never telling anyone where they are?

Part of me wonders if this is dangerous. I am moving to a community of werewolves. I didn't even know that they existed before yesterday. Now, not only do I need to accept that they are real, but I also have to entrust my life to them.

Bo texts me back that we can meet at his hotel whenever I am ready.

I realize that he is trying to be gentle with me after shocking me to the point of fainting yesterday, but I want to get on with it. I need answers, and I need to get to work. It's what I do, and honestly, it's all I have.

I'll be moving to a community about which I know very little. What I do know is that it's close-knit, but I'm not sure how that will work out for me. Maybe they will be friendly and welcome me with open arms like Bo's advisory team did. Or maybe they will be suspicious of a newcomer.

If I am being honest with myself, I don't know which I prefer. If they welcome me, it will make the work easier, but I don't know how to maintain lasting friendships. This will be my first time living in a community for more than a few years. I'm supposed to stay with Bo's people forever.

For the first time in my life, I will be setting down roots. And those roots will be in a community where I am not just an outsider, but a different species. Had I known the truth before I agreed to the assignment, would I have done it?

It is an impossible question to answer.

There is definitely a thrill to the unknown. I am excited to tackle problems that I never could have dreamed of in a normal diplomatic life. I am excited to learn about a culture and religion that almost no other humans in the world know exist. I will also be able to step outside of my normal role to work with law enforcement and hospitals. Who knows the different types of roles I'll need to step into over the next 40 years or so?

Can I really do this? Can I spend 40 years in the same town with the same people doing the same job?

I understand that most people do exactly that. They live and die in the same place where they were born. They work in the same job, sometimes in the same office, for decades.

Surely, I can handle this. At least my job requires travel, and there is hardly ever monotony. It's always something different—different people, different problems, unique situations.

I guess I'd better get dressed and start the day, Bo and my future are waiting.

※

When I arrive at Bo's suite, he is waiting with coffee and breakfast foods.

"How did you sleep?" He asks as we make our way to the sitting area.

I turn around slightly to smile at him, "I actually slept pretty well. I think I was exhausted."

"Good," he says. "Is there anywhere in particular that you want to start today?"

Nodding, I say, "Yes, before we get into anything else, can we nail down my relocation details?"

Bo looks physically relieved.

"What did you think I was going to say?" I ask.

Bo scratches the back of his head and looks towards my feet. "I don't know, but I was hoping that you didn't decide to quit. I know this is a lot. Before yesterday, you were sure that I was just a man and that my people were just normal humans who lived simple lives."

I smile as sweetly as I can muster, "You underestimate me. I am committed to my duties as your ambassador. I take my role and my obligations very seriously. I may not understand everything, and I may have freaked out a little bit yesterday, but that doesn't change anything. I am still dedicated to making this world a better place. And last I checked, Oregon was still a part of this world."

"Well then," Bo says with a wide, boyish smile. "Let's get started."

Initially, Bo had wanted to give me two weeks to pack my belongings and have them shipped out. But once I explained how minimalist my life is, we decided that I would join him in Oregon this Friday.

Eventually, I will have my own home near Bo's. However, until I am comfortable in my new community, I will stay in Bo's home. I want to ask him if he has a wife or girlfriend at home, but I also feel like it might send the wrong message. Surely, if he hasn't mentioned someone yet, then there isn't, right?

I don't know, I guess I'll find out soon enough, though.

We will fly in the community's private plane directly to their land. I will be paid my ambassador salary from the U.S. government, but my home and car will be provided by Bo. I'll also have access to their community grocery and kitchen services if I wish to use them.

Deliveries from outside, online retailers are made to the postal depot on the edge of Ulfserkir land, transported into the city, and delivered by community postal workers. The added stop can delay deliveries by a day, but usually, they are very fast.

There are also many stores located in the city center, selling everything from pastries to furniture. They even have cell phone stores.

Aside from the lack of tall buildings and hotels, it is exactly like any normal American town. But, full of werewolves.

"How's the signal strength out there?" I ask, holding up my cell phone.

"It is surprisingly strong," Bo says. "We have great internet speed, too. I promise that you'll have all the comforts of home."

I laugh, "You realize that I have lived all over the world, right? When I was 11, we lived in a mud hut for 3 months."

"I mean," Bo says with a shrug, "if that is what you want, I can ask the construction crew to change gears."

I am relieved that, after yesterday's heavy revelations, Bo and I have fallen back into our normal, casual, and friendly banter. He is really very easy to talk to and work alongside.

As a rule, I usually don't get too attached to my diplomatic charges. They are clients, not friends. Plus, I will be out of their lives in a few months, maybe a year at most. But this assignment is different. I will be with Bo for as long as he is in power, and even after that, we will still be neighbors.

"How do you think your people will react to me?" I finally blurt out.

Bo leans back in his chair and makes his "thinking hard" face. "I think most people will be excited to meet you like Chester, Candy, and Roman were. We have our own news stations, so the community knows that you are coming and that you are human. Even with 300,000 people in the central city, you probably won't have to introduce yourself. We do have citizens who have never met a human, and there are people who have had bad experiences with humans. So, some people might be a little more wary than others."

"That's actually pretty standard when I travel to a new assignment," I shrug. "At least we don't have to tackle a language barrier. So, hurray for small victories."

Oh no, Bo tilted his head. He is curious again.

"I'll say it again, Ellie, I am very impressed by you." He says. "You are handling this really well. I almost feel like I should be worried.

I expected fear or disgust. Even anger. But you are just going with the flow as if this is a normal assignment."

"I spent a lot of time thinking about what you said yesterday about power and fear, and how we react to anyone different from us," I say. "I have spent my entire life preaching the equality of all people. I have worked in war-torn countries, and I've listened to stories of whole families wiped out because they belong to a different religion or were born with a different skin color than their neighbor. How could I look myself in the mirror if I became that? If I fell into the bigotry that I have fought against my whole life, then what am I even doing here?"

"You are a remarkable woman," Bo says with a big fat smile and warmth that feels somehow, intimate.

Chapter Nine

Bo and I exit the plane at the small Ulfserkir airfield. He couldn't believe it when I showed up to board with just four suitcases and a duffle bag.

For the trip, I wore sneakers, jeans, and a sweater. No one likes to fly in a suit and high heels.

When we reach the bottom of the stairs, I see Roman has come to pick us up in a large black SUV. Bo carries three of my suitcases, while I shoulder the duffle bag and pull one suitcase behind me.

Roman runs over to me, taking my bags while simultaneously wrapping me into a warm embrace. He motions toward the plane, "How many more on board? Will we need another truck? Or did you ship the rest?"

Bo shakes his head, "Believe it or not, Roman, this is it."

Turning to face me, Roman says, "Are you kidding me, young lady? I have never seen a woman travel so lightly. My wife takes more than this on a week-long vacation."

I laugh as I watch him load my bags into the back of the SUV. "I moved around a lot my whole life. You learn to live lean."

Roman motions for me to sit in the front passenger seat, Bo gets into the driver's seat, and the giant bear-sized man climbs into the back seat behind Bo.

"You don't have to sit in the back, Roman," I say. "I can get back there."

"Nonsense," he replies. "Besides, Bo will drop me off at home on the way. No need to shuffle around when we get there. By the way, don't be surprised if my wife is waiting outside. I told her that we would get the chance to have you over for dinner after you have settled in a bit, but she's pretty damn eager to meet you and roll out the welcome wagon."

Bo laughs. "I would expect nothing less from Francine. To be honest, I was half expecting her to jump out of the car when we got here."

"I had to sneak out while she was in the kitchen," Roman adds. "I'm in for an earful when you two leave."

We all laugh, and soon the two men are talking shop.

"Anything important happen since we spoke yesterday?" Bo asks.

Roman's face suddenly takes on a downtrodden appearance. "Jasper called; he's got some trouble to discuss with you, but wanted to wait until you were back in the office to talk about it."

I'm not sure who Jasper is, but Bo seems concerned with the news. I almost ask about it, but decide that I'll hold off for now. I don't want to pry and overstep my bounds before I've even gotten started.

It doesn't take us long to start seeing farm homes. These must be the homesteaders that Bo talked about; people who live in the community borders but outside of the main city. As we drive, Bo and Roman point out the different homes and talk about the families who live there. Some they know personally, others by reputation.

Even though the homesteaders live outside the city, they still supply the pack with wool, produce, honey, milk, and meat. Although they live more solitary lives day to day, they are still heavily involved in the community overall.

As we approach the outskirts of the city, the homes become closer together, but many still have gardens overflowing with vegetables and brightly colored flowers. I can see children and adults outside playing in yards.

Even as we enter the city, the homes are still spaced apart with green grass and trees between them. There aren't many fences separating the properties. I suppose it is because the land is community-owned, and neighbors treat it that way.

The city looks like an idyllic suburban paradise. If it weren't for the occasional strip mall, I would think this place was a fake 1950s T.V. neighborhood from one of those old family shows.

As we reach the center of the city, I can see what I assume is the business district. There are factories and warehouses, but they are all clean and well-maintained. It is amazing what a city can look like when the citizens have a stake in it and take pride in keeping it beautiful.

The north half of the city looks much the same as the southern half: houses of various sizes and shapes, children running through the yards, and people walking to and from stores.

After a while, we pull down a side street and then onto a cul-de-sac. There is a middle-aged woman in a long flowy skirt and button-down blouse standing at the edge of a driveway and I can only assume that it is Francine Bernulf.

Roman immediately sits up straighter in his seat. Yup, that's his wife.

Bo parks the SUV in front of Francine and turns to me while he unbuckles his seatbelt. "We better say a quick hello," he says. "It might be the only thing that saves Roman from a lashing."

I laugh and join him in getting out of the SUV. Roman is already out of the car and scurrying to his wife's side.

"Hello, my dear," he says and leans down to kiss her cheek. She simply side-eyes him. "I would like to introduce you to Eloise Margrave."

"Please," I say, extending my hand to her, "call me Ellie."

"It is so nice to," Francine side-eyes Roman again, "*finally,* meet you. Roman spoke so highly of you." As Francine takes my hand, I can see her wrinkle her nose. Gazing between Bo and her husband, she adds, "They didn't tell me nearly enough about you."

We spend a few minutes exchanging pleasantries and promising to have dinner together before Bo and I climb back into the SUV and get back on the road.

"Do I smell funny?" I ask when we are a short distance from the house.

Bo seems put off by the question, so I elaborate. "It's just that Francine crinkled her nose after taking my hand and then looked at you two like you had done something wrong."

"Um," Bo says, making a strange face. "How do I put this? Um, first, you don't smell bad. Sorry, I know that's important to girls, women, I mean, people. Ugh, this is weird to explain. You smell nicer than most humans do."

"OK," I say, confused but relieved that I don't stink. "I guess I can live with that. Better than smelling bad, right? I have another question. Do all your advisors live close to each other? Or are you all spread out?"

Bo glances at me with a relieved look on his face, then returns his attention to the road in front of him. "We are pretty spread out. We have an office that we work from in the city center a few days a week. If we need to meet on the weekend, we use my house. I have a conference room that can hold 15 people, but we usually just sit around the fireplace in the living room. We aren't as formal and flashy as your government. My people can come right to our offices or show up at my door with an issue."

We talk for a while about the type of issues they have in the pack lands. Most are logistical in nature. Do they need more roads, mail trucks, and parking garages? What type of storefront should they encourage people to open? Are the schools properly supplied?

Sometimes, the matters are more serious. Recently, Bo had to send members of their "police" force to look for a missing postgraduate student attending college out of state. Turns out that she had gone for a wolf run and gotten caught up in a poacher's snare. She was able to break the snare free of the tree, but it was wrapped around her tightly. Trapped in her wolf form, she was stuck in the woods.

They got her free and brought her back to school. A quick fake doctor's note got her back on track with her teachers, and all was well again.

"How does your police force work?" I ask.

Bo explains that they are a volunteer squad that attends a boot camp modeled after the U.S. military. They are also the same soldiers that the government calls on for top secret missions.

"What do they do most of the time?" I ask. "You said before that you don't have a lot of crime."

Bo nods in agreement. "That's right, we don't. Most days, they travel around the community borders checking for signs of poachers. They stop in and visit with some of our more remote homesteaders to make sure they are OK. There is the occasional lost child who needs tracking. Mostly, they are just available to the community to lend a hand with farm work, cattle wrangling, or car troubles. Whatever is needed, really."

"So," I say, "they just serve the community however they can?"

Bo nods. "Yeah. Whatever they can do to help. They've even babysat older kids while their baby siblings are being born. We don't even call them police; they're the Pack Squad. They protect the pack and keep it strong."

"How did you build a community of 600,000 people who don't need a police force?" I ask, looking out the window of the car at the picturesque town.

"That's actually the easy part," Bo says. "We modeled our community after the Ulfheðnar's way of life instead of the human way. Our people don't have to worry about keeping a roof over their family's heads or putting food on the table. Those are the biggest stressors in the human world. So many of your people are working multiple jobs just to afford to live. Or they live in squalor like stray animals. Then, when they see people who work less but have more, they get angry. Or maybe they just give up. Either way, it divides your people. You have rich people stepping over starving children. Middle-class people killing themselves at jobs they hate. And everyone turns to drugs and alcohol to cope with the pain. Crime and violence always follow pain and misery."

He isn't wrong about that. Bo's community is set up like a profit-sharing co-op. Everyone works to keep it running because everyone benefits from it. Who benefits from our hard work in the human world?

As we leave the city behind, the houses are beginning to thin out.

"How much further to your house?" I ask Bo.

He motions ahead of us to the left. "It's just up there. That one on the hill. I have a housekeeper who also cooks for me. Her name is Janeal, and she would usually be gone by now, but I would guess that she is still there. You're kinda big news around here, and everyone wants to catch a glimpse."

I take in the sight of Bo's home. It looks straight out of a painting. It's beautiful, with two stories, off-white siding with dark green shutters around the windows, and a large wrap-around porch. Straight, old-school Americana.

※

Bo was correct, Janeal is waiting on the porch when we arrive. She smiles a little too widely at Bo when he gets out of the SUV, like a child who snuck cookies from the cookie jar.

She used the excuse of wanting to help me settle into my new room, but we all knew that she was really just dying of curiosity.

I decide to indulge her and ask if she wants to help me hang up my clothes. She greedily takes two suitcases from Bo and runs ahead of me to show me the way to my room.

Janeal turns to the right at the top of the stairs. As I reach the top, I can see five doors: one just to the left of the stairs, another door 10 feet down from that, and then another facing me at the end of the hall.

To the right, I see one door along the hallway and another facing me at the end. Janeal tells me that the doors at either end of the hall are mine (to the right) and Bo's (to the left). They are both master suites with en-suite bathrooms and walk-in closets. The other doors are two guest rooms and a jack-and-jill bathroom that sits between them.

The walls and doors are all painted the same shade of hunter green. The trim is stained wood, and the ceiling is cream-colored. All the doors in the house have lever-style handles. I wonder if it is so that they can open the doors in their wolf form.

"No pets or kids, huh?" I say to Janeal, gesturing down to the pristinely clean carpeting running up the stairs and along the hallway.

Janeal raises her eyebrows at me, "You didn't know that Bo is single. Didn't you two just spend an entire week getting to know each other?"

I shrug my shoulders. "I didn't ask, and he never mentioned. It's not really my place to pry into his private life. I'm just an ambassador, and he is a client."

"Are you married?" she asks. Apparently, completely oblivious to what I've just said about not prying.

"No," I say with a smile. "I have always traveled too much. And now I'm here, so I guess that ship has sailed."

Janeal makes a slightly frowning face. "Yeah, I guess so. I mean, surely, they could make an exception for you, though." She says as she is flipping open my bags.

Before I have a chance to question her on what that means, she puts her hands on her hips and turns to face me.

"Are these all of your clothes?" She says in a high-pitched, shocked voice.

From behind me, I hear Bo's voice. "Oh, no, Janeal. She has a duffle bag too."

Turning, I yell down the hall, "Actually, smarty-pants, that bag is full of yoga gear."

Janeal lets out a burst of laughter. "Well, I guess I'll have to take you into town for some shopping. We have some really nice clothing stores in the city center. We'll get you stocked up. You barely have enough to fill half a rack in the closet."

Walking into the closet, I realize that it is the size of a New York City apartment. "Wow, this is great. I can set this up as a yoga room."

This time, when I hear Bo's voice, it is right behind me. "No way. You are not doing yoga in the closet. I already had the guest room next door set up as an office for you; you can do your yoga in there. This is for your clothes and storage for anything you want to pick up for your new house."

Chapter Ten

We are 3 hours behind Washington D.C., so it is still early evening by the time I unpack and settle in. I'm dead tired, but I know that I must stay up a while longer to acclimate to the time change quickly.

To be honest, 3 hours isn't so bad, and I find it easier to go back in time rather than forward. It's easier for me to stay awake when I'm tired than to sleep when I'm not.

I head downstairs to see the rest of the house. The lower floor is much larger than the second floor. There are the standard rooms, living room, dining room, and kitchen. There's a guest bathroom between the kitchen and living room.

Toward the back of the house, there is a large addition. This is where the conference room and Bo's office are. There is another bathroom back there as well.

The style is very modern. The kitchen is designed with gorgeous, I think they are quartz counters and clean lines. A large apron sink gives it a contemporary farmhouse feel. It's surprisingly cozy.

I find myself mulling around the kitchen. Janeal told me earlier that there was food waiting for me in the refrigerator. I open the refrigerator door and find it full of pre-cooked, ready-to-heat meals.

I guess that is very convenient for a busy bachelor.

While I look through the meals, I hear Bo coming down the stairs. He is freshly showered and has a peppy bounce in his step.

"You sure are happy to be home," I say.

"You have no idea," he says, reaching around me and grabbing a meal. His body is just inches from mine, and the casual closeness has my nerves on edge. He doesn't seem the least bit phased by the proximity of his chest to my back.

"We have heightened senses," he continues. "Even when we are in our human form, so being in a city like that for so long really starts to wear me down. It's so noisy with all the traffic and people right on top of each other. And it reeks of garbage and piss."

"Sounds lovely," I say. "I guess I'd be happy to be out of there, too."

Bo wrinkles his nose in disgust and shakes his head. Until he just mentioned it, I hadn't realized just how quiet it really is here. I can see why he would miss this place.

"I'm going to make a quick call from the back office," Bo says. "But then I'll be out to eat dinner if you want to join me."

"Sure," I say. "I was just thinking about eating some dinner too. I'll heat up a couple of plates and meet you at the table."

Bo retreats to the back of the house and into his office. I notice that he doesn't bother shutting the door. I guess I'll be privy to most of his private business soon anyway, so why bother?

 I can only vaguely make out the conversation. Sounds like he is calling Jasper back, the man Roman mentioned in the car earlier.

I turn my attention back to the dinners. They have instructions on the lid.

Oven: 350 - 25 mins

REMOVE LID!

Instantly, I envision the leader of 800,000 people putting a plastic lid into the oven and not realizing that it will melt all over his food. I guess men are men, no matter how far they climb the ladder or what they can shapeshift into.

I turn on the oven and pop the meals inside. I take an educated guess that Janeal knew that a man like Bo doesn't wait for the oven to preheat before putting the food in. If he can't figure out that he has to remove the lid, he probably hasn't figured out the preheating.

After a few minutes, Bo returns to the kitchen. "We are going to have a guest for a few days, maybe more. His name is Jasper

Adolpha, and he is the leader of the German pack and sort of the King of the shifter community as a whole. He's got an issue that he needs my help with. I was hoping to give you more time to settle in before getting involved in anything like this, but I guess Luna had other ideas."

I lift my eyebrows at him, "Luna?"

Bo scrunches his face in thought. "Um, yeah, you don't really know about our goddess. Luna is the goddess who oversees the Ulfheðnar. In this realm, you have your Divine creator, Jehovah, who you very creatively refer to as God. But your creator isn't the only creator. There is an entire race of divine beings, there are higher divine beings who oversee their own realms, and minor divine beings who assist with the management of those realms. Luna oversees the Ulfheðnar and watches over us as well. She is represented in this realm by your moon."

I take a moment to digest this new information. I was never very religious, but it makes sense. I have been all over the world, this world anyway, and there are many different beliefs, but they all pretty much boil down to the same core structure.

"Interesting." It's all I really have to say about it.

Bo continues. "Anyway, Jasper has a problem with a rogue wolf. He thinks that his guy has traveled to the U.S. So, he is going to fly in tomorrow to start the search here."

"Wow," I say, bringing the food to the table. "That does sound like a problem. Do we know anything about him or what he did in Germany?"

Bo shakes his head. "Not a lot, Jasper will fill us in when he gets here tomorrow. I know he is charged with murder, but I don't know the details."

While I take my seat at the table, Bo grabs a bottle of wine from the small wine refrigerator built into the kitchen island. He brings the wine and two glasses to the table.

As we drink and eat, we fall into conversation.

I learned that werewolf children usually change for the first time around age 6, though some have been known to change as early as 4 if they get really scared.

All wolf children are required to either attend a pack school or be homeschooled if they live outside of the pack land. It is too hard for young children to control their wolf instincts when they change, and even harder for them to suppress the urge to 'shift' when they are upset.

According to Bo, most families with young children stay on or close to pack lands so the community can help the family through those first few years while a child learns to access their wolf form and control their instincts.

"It's really nice how the community comes together to help each other," I say. "It's so different from other large communities. It's more like a small village atmosphere. It's hard to believe that there is a large city like this where everyone just helps each other."

"It has gotten harder in recent years," Bo says. "The internet has brought a lot of negative influence to the community. It was easier when the kids and young adults only knew this way of life. They just naturally accepted that neighbors help each other and that the pack is stronger together. Now they are bombarded with social media influencers telling them that they should be selfish and materialistic."

"How are you countering that," I ask, unable to stop myself from slipping into problem-solving mode.

"It's an ongoing battle," Bo says. "For a while, some of the older pack members wanted to block the internet. But we can't stop progress. We can't shelter our kids from the world. We have to teach them why we live this way and show them the truth of what greed does to a community. We've added lessons to the school curriculum that talk about Internet deceit and scams."

"That's a good strategy," I say. "When you try to hide something, it just makes it that much more appealing. Knowledge really is power.

You can't shield them from everything, but you can arm them with the truth and prepare them for what's out there."

"It's working," Bo says. "Only a small percentage of our young people leave the pack lands for the outside world. And an even smaller percentage stay out there."

I take a sip of my wine and nod. "I can imagine that it's quite a shock to move from the security of pack life into the rat race of our world. I'd move back too."

Bo laughs, "Well, you live here now."

"That reminds me," I say. "Janeal asked if I could go shopping with her tomorrow. Do you mind if we head into town? She says my wardrobe is too small and that I don't have any ranch clothes."

Bo tilts his head. "You don't need my permission to do anything. If you want to go out with Janeal, then please, take one of the cars and have a great time. I mean, you do drive, right?"

I toss a small piece of dinner roll at his face, which he catches in his mouth. I'm immediately shocked at myself. I just threw food at the leader of a sovereign nation. This isn't a couple of friends having dinner, this is my brand-new boss.

I quickly pull myself together.

"Yes, I can drive. I just wanted to make sure you didn't have anything planned for me," I say. "We haven't really discussed your expectations of me or what hours you would like me to be available, plus you said that Jasper would be flying in tomorrow and I am unsure what that means for my work schedule."

Bo shakes his head. "You aren't expected to revolve your life here around me. Right now, I just want you to get acquainted with the community, learn the city, and meet some people. Get comfortable with your new home. We can set up office hours for you when you have a better idea of what you want your schedule to be."

OK, so he isn't mad about the food-based assault.

And he doesn't want to set my hours for me.

Interesting.

※

After I wake and brush my teeth, I text Janeal and asked if she still wants to go shopping. She immediately responds that she can pick me up in two hours. It's hard not to smile at her eagerness to show me around.

While I wait for Janeal, I shower, get dressed, and head downstairs for breakfast.

I find Bo standing at the kitchen island, drinking coffee and looking at his phone.

"Good morning," I say, rounding the island and heading to the coffee maker. It is one of those single-cup makers that uses the little pods. I pop one in the top and grab a cup from the rack. "Is everything OK?"

Bo looks up from his phone and smiles, "Yup, just checking with Jasper about his flight plan. He took off a few hours ago and should be here in about seven more hours. He'll let me know when he's close, and I'll head back to the airstrip. What about you? Did you get ahold of Janeal?"

I laugh. "I'm pretty sure she was holding her phone all morning waiting for me to text her. She should be here in about a half hour to pick me up. Gotta get me those rancher clothes. She said you have some livestock and that I can't be wearing my fancy clothes out in the fields with the animals."

Bo laughs as well. "That sounds like her. We do have some steers, chickens, goats, and even a couple of alpacas. But I think she really just wants to be the one to take you around and introduce you to everyone. She's excited to have a woman around here and really wants to make sure that you're comfortable."

OK, so not a lot of women in Bo's house. Another small piece of information to file away. Not that I have any kind of feeling one way or the other about the number of women who breeze through Bo's house or how long they hang around. I'm just gathering all the facts so that I can build a good working model of this community in my mind. It's my job to notice and understand these things.

OK, so I might slightly appreciate the fact that there hasn't been a parade of women marching through Bo's house. That doesn't mean anything, though. I am just happy that he has a better character than that. That's all.

"Well, I definitely need some more casual clothes," I say. "Based off what I've observed about you, jeans and t-shirts are the uniform around here."

Bo raises an eyebrow. "So, you've been observing me, huh?"

Oh shit.

"No! I mean, it's my job to blend in with my new community," I say in a high pitch while rolling my eyes at him. I quickly turn my back to him and continue on. "It'll be nice to buy clothes without worrying about how heavy they'll be in a suitcase. And there's no use waiting to get out there and start meeting people. Janeal and I will probably shop for a few hours, then do lunch, and then I'll head back here. I want to get my office equipment set up tonight and get through some of my reading materials."

I realize that I am starting to ramble and cut myself off.

It's not a lie, though. The Secretary of State provided me with a ton of procedure documents and a lengthy treaty to read through. It's important for me to understand the responsibilities of the U.S. government and the Ulfserkir community under the treaty agreement between us.

It'll be my job to make sure that the treaty is upheld by both sides.

JL Thompson

Chapter Eleven

Janeal and I have a great day shopping. She takes me to her favorite stores. We are just about the same size, so her style of clothing actually fits me fairly well. She and I look similar, but she has bright blonde hair cut in a cute, layered bob just below her ears. She also has about 2 inches on me, making her maybe 5'10" tall.

She is so bubbly and happy. It's absolutely refreshing to be around someone like her after being surrounded by the vultures and snakes in Washington D.C.

Janeal introduces me to everyone she can, including workers inside the stores, other customers, and even people on the street as we walk. So far, everyone has been just as nice as Janeal.

Everyone here seems so happy and genuinely glad to meet a new person, even someone different from them. It's kind of weird.

I feel like I'm in a dream world. Can this be a real place? Is it possible that, with only a few key changes in the system, you can create a world where people actually love and help their neighbors? Can it really be that simple? Or is it the genetic differences between us that contribute to this idyllic society that the wolf walkers have created?

It's getting close to lunchtime, and I ask Janeal where we should go. She suggests a small cafe around the corner from the store we're currently at. Not surprisingly, she knows the owner and would love to introduce me to him.

We finish up in the dressing rooms, and I decide on three new pairs of jeans and some really nice cotton t-shirts. I add this bag to my already overstuffed arms. I also bought new leggings, bras, underwear, sweatshirts, sweaters, and now jeans and t-shirts. I bought more clothes today than I have in the last five years combined.

After we check out, we head to the corner cafe. The huge windows make it brightly lit inside. There are about a dozen tables inside and another five or six set up out front of the cafe.

Janeal walks in ahead of me and greets the young girl behind the counter. She introduces me to her. Apparently, her name is Tracy, and her family owns the cafe. Her father runs it and cooks in the back.

The girl yells through the kitchen door, and a man who hardly looks old enough to have a working-aged daughter appears. Janeal introduces me to the man, Stanley. After a few moments of pleasantries, we are seated and treated to a chef's special lunch, on the house.

Stanley insists on treating us to lunch as a welcome to the community.

While we wait, Janeal and I fall into conversation.

"Stanley looks way too young to be Tracy's father," I say.

Janeal smirks before replying. "We age a little slower than you are used to. For instance, I am 55 years old."

My jaw falls open, I would have guessed Janeal to be in her mid-30s. "Wow, you look my age."

Janeal poses with her hands under her chin like a 1950s pin-up girl, and we both laugh.

She explains to me that since they are partly of the Ulfheðnar realm, where time moves much, much slower, they enjoy the benefit of a longer lifespan and slower aging.

Apparently, Roman is almost 100 years old. I would have guessed him in his 60s. And that is more because of the way he carries himself than his actual physical appearance. In a photo, he might pass for early 50s.

"We live around 200 years," Janeal explains. "But just like you, we can die younger or live longer than normal. I had an aunt that made it to 227 years old."

"Holy shit," I say. "How old is Bo?"

Janeal wags her eyebrows up and down suggestively. "Want to make sure he's not too old for you, huh?"

"No," I say a little too sharply to be convincing. "I just don't know that I can trust my assessments anymore. He could be 30 or he could be 70. I'm just curious."

"Sure," she says, rolling her eyes at me. "We'll go with that. Anyway, Bo, who you totally aren't interested in at all, is 45."

"Bo is my client," I say, hopefully in a more convincing tone this time. "I'm an ambassador, it is completely inappropriate for me to have interest in him outside of work. It's a conflict of interest."

"Good," she says. "Because he has a girlfriend who is out of town right now but will be back in a few days."

"Oh," I say in a way too high-pitched voice. "I didn't know that."

My face must have betrayed me because Janeal broke into an ear-to-ear smile and quickly said, "Ha, I knew it. You were jealous. He doesn't have a girlfriend. How could you possibly think that there has been a woman in that house!"

I scowl at Janeal but laugh despite myself. "I was not jealous; I was just shocked because we spent a lot of time together talking over the last week, and he never mentioned anything about a girlfriend. It's the kind of information I would have expected him to share with me since I am staying in his house. That's all. But you are right, that house is definitely not feminine at all."

Janeal looks utterly unconvinced. This is dangerous territory, so I decide to change the subject.

"Can I ask you a kind of personal question?" I ask.

"No problem," Janeal says with a smile. "I'll give you the rundown on every date Bo has had in the last 5 years."

I roll my eyes at her. "No, I don't care about that. I want to know more about what it's like to, you know, when you change."

"Oooooh," Janeal says. "Sure, ask me whatever you want. I'm not sure that I'll have all the scientific answers or whatever, but I'll do my best."

We spend the next hour or so talking about how she shifts and what it feels like. She says it doesn't really hurt, but feels like your bones are popping, like cracking knuckles, but extreme. She says that some wolves, really strong-blooded ones, can learn to shift just certain parts of themselves at a time.

"It is extremely rare," Janeal says. "I have never seen a wolf will themselves to partially shift with my own eyes. But I have heard rumors that Bo has done it."

"When you are young," she says. "You sometimes don't shift all the way. It's very awkward. Uncomfortable but not really painful. We teach the youngins to focus on being a wolf and imagining themselves changing. I can't really explain it, but it's like there is a switch inside us that lets us change from human to wolf and back. It's hard for the kids to change back sometimes because, as a wolf they get overwhelmed with the smells and sensations. Sometimes the urge to take off to the woods is too strong, and they just run for it. Then, we call the kittens in to help find them."

I look at her with wide eyes, "I'm sorry, the what?"

"The kittens," she says with a laugh. "It's a little nickname we have for the Pack Squad. Their initials are PS, like psss psss psss. The way you would call a kitten. Plus, they are all cute and helpful until they have to let out their claws, then they might tear you to shreds."

We both laugh at the idea of the pack's police force being called the kittens.

"Why are people so eager to meet me," I ask.

Janeal shrugs before answering. "You have to understand that most of us don't interact with a lot of humans throughout our lives. And when we do, they are usually awful greed monsters. When we heard you were coming and that you were approved by Bo, everyone was excited. You're like a unicorn amongst humans."

"I am totally confused," I tell her. "I understood the words, but I have no idea what they mean. What makes me so special compared to any other human?"

"OK, so you know we have better senses than humans, right?" She asks. "Even in our human form, we can scent people. Everyone has their own scent, that's how your tracking dogs can use scent to find a specific person. What tracking dogs can't tell you is that people's scents are affected by their emotions and desires. Greed, power lust, and basically bad intentions make a person's smell take on an essence of rot, like garbage. Anxiety and fear heighten their scent. Happiness adds sweetness to it. Someone who is always acting in their own interests at the expense of other people or is ruled by greed becomes stained with that rot smell over time. And sadly, most humans carry that stench. Bo wasn't too keen on bringing a stinky human to pack lands. We were all pretty sure that he would never find someone that he could tolerate."

"Really," I say, utterly shocked by this revelation. "Is that why Bo says that Washington D.C. smelled like garbage and piss? Everyone there is ruled by greed and desire for power."

"Yeah," she says, making a sour face. "I bet it reeks. Ugh. This also brings me back to why Bo doesn't date. Bo has even keener senses than most wolves. It's been hard for him to go on more than a few dates before a woman starts to get that rotten smell. When he starts to pick up the hint of rot or sourness, he realizes that the woman doesn't like him as much as she is pretending; she just wants to be the one to marry the alpha and produce the next generation of alphas. They don't mean to deceive him, and they probably don't even realize it themselves. But he can't ignore it."

I feel like I am on information overload. I am not sure what to focus on: the fact that Bo rarely dates or the idea that I smell like a good person. My heart chooses for me, and I suddenly start to feel bad for Bo. It must be hard to realize that someone you genuinely like is less interested in you than they are in your position.

"That's terrible," I say. "Bo told me that you have a hierarchy, but that it isn't as divided as humans."

"Yeah," Janeal says. "The Alpha is the top of the pack, his council of advisors are below him, the Pack Squad are below them, and the rest of the pack are below them. But the entire pack has a say in how the pack is run. Any one of us can knock on Bo's door and talk to him about what is on our minds, make suggestions, or ask for help. There isn't a big divide between the Alpha and the pack. Bo lives in the outskirts of the city, the council members live in different areas around the city, and they keep an office in the center of the city. This way, they are spread out in every corner of the town, and easily accessible by any pack member. They keep their eyes on their neighborhoods and know what is going on in their areas. The Pack Squad makes sure to visit the families that live farther outside of town and make sure that they are OK and still feel connected to the pack."

"So, if Bo isn't living like a king, why do the women smell power hungry," I say, "I mean, it's clearly not for wealth, so is it respect then, or maybe out of duty to further the pack and be the next Alpha's mother. I guess I can see how women here might almost feel obligated to continue the relationship to make their pack stronger."

"Yup," Janeal says. "They might not even realize that they feel that way, but their scent can't be ignored. Most women in the pack want a pack husband. Someone who works local, is home every night to help with the kids, and takes care of the house."

Janeal looks over at me with raised eyebrows. "Bo isn't that man. He is worldly and travels all the time, and he has been taking care of himself for a long time. Bo isn't the kind of man who is looking for a wife to take care of him; he wants a partner who can talk to him and offer him advice. Someone who knows a lot about the world, but still wants to learn more. I mean, where could he ever find a woman like that, Ellie?"

I roll my eyes again. "I told you, Janeal, Bo is my client, and that is all. I won't deny that I like him as a person. He is very easy to talk to, but it's nothing more than that. I'm sure he feels the same way. Besides, I am just a human woman. I can't compete with a werewolf woman. I'll never be able to understand you guys fully. I will always just be a single being inside of a single body."

"Oh, please," Janeal rolls her eyes at me now. "Girl, who cares? I have already seen him show more interest in you than he has in any woman, ever. And I only saw you two interact for what, two hours."

"He just wants me to feel comfortable so that I don't freak out and quit," I say. "It's not what you think, I promise. Besides, look around Janeal. You all look like fitness models. I'm nothing special in the human world, and I really blend into the walls around here."

Janeal waves her hand at me. "You're crazy girl. You look amazing. Don't ever feel like you aren't beautiful, because I'm here to tell you that more than one head has turned today, and they already know what I look like. Besides, Bo isn't so shallow. I'll say this last thing, the women he has dated haven't followed a physical type. They have been all over the board. He is much more interested in who you are than what you look like."

"That's amazing," I say, "and not at all surprising. But, who I am, is human."

While I appreciate Janeal's confidence in me, I'm positive that I don't have the kind of appeal that even human world leaders are looking for in a wife—more like a secretary.

Bo is a whole different animal...literally. Yes, he is very friendly with me, but so was Stanley. Does that mean that Stanley is into me too? No. It means that this community is a friendly one and the people here are exceptional at making newcomers feel welcomed. As their leader, it stands to reason that Bo would be the person trying the hardest to make me feel welcomed.

No doubt, Bo and I will be great friends. And one day, if I'm lucky, I'll stand at his wedding and play with his kids. His very wolfy wedding with his very wolfy kids.

Chapter Twelve

Once I am back at Bo's house, I decide to change into my yoga gear. Bo will be gone for the day. My plan is simple, I'll set up the office, do some heavy reading, then get some yoga in. I haven't done any kind of stretching in days and it is starting to make me feel out of balance.

As promised, Bo has cleared the room of bedroom furniture and left only a desk, complete with everything I need to set up a comfortable workstation. Bo has also set up a small refrigerator full of water bottles. I'm momentarily taken aback by the thoughtfulness of the gesture.

I'll have to do something nice for Bo as a thank you. I have no idea what, but I'm sure I'll come up with something. Maybe Janeal can help me out.

I get straight to work. Setting up the laptop is easy since Bo already set up the monitor, keyboard, and mouse. I basically just have to plug it all in, and I am ready to go. There is a note on the desk with the Wi-Fi information.

In a matter of minutes, I am sorting through legal documents and even starting to skim through the 127-page treaty. I don't make it too far into the treaty before I see an addendum about human/wolf marriage and another regarding "artificial heir production."

I make a mental note, I'll have to come back to that later.

It's time to pop in my noise-canceling earbuds, start my favorite meditation mix, and hit my yoga mat.

I'm not sure how long I've been going for, but I am drenched in sweat. Without removing my earbuds, I grab a bottle of water from the refrigerator. I head to the guest bathroom since it is connected to the office.

Without thinking twice, I whip open the door and find a naked man in a towel.

Startled, I let out a scream and jump backward. The man is holding up his hands in surrender and speaking, but I can't hear him with my earbuds still playing my meditation mix.

I scramble to remove them as Bo comes bursting into the room as well.

The man is still holding up his hands in surrender when Bo enters, and just as his eyes take in the scene, the towel falls to the floor. I am so stunned that it takes me a moment to realize that I need to turn around.

I finally get my earbuds out, and I can hear the men now. Bo is yelling at the man and demanding to know what is going on. The man is laughing and teasing Bo about buying bigger towels.

I interrupt the argument by yelling, "I'm so sorry. I had my earbuds in, and I lost track of time, and I was sweaty, and I didn't know anyone was here. Oh my God, I'm so sorry. I'm so embarrassed. I'm going to go to my room now and die of shame. Bye."

With that, I slam the door to the bathroom and run to my room. I immediately head for my own bathroom and close the door behind me.

I can't believe I just did that. How stupid can I be? That had to be Jasper. The damn leader of the German Ulfheðnar people and, you know, King of the wolf walkers. I just saw him naked. Before I even so much as introduced myself to him, I barged in on him while he was naked. Then, I had the audacity to gawk at his naked body.

Can you die of embarrassment? Because if you can, I am sure that this is how that happens.

I have been in this house for like 26 hours, and I have already thrown food at the face of one leader and barged into the shower of another. What the hell is happening to me?

Way to go, Ellie! I am crushing it at being an ambassador. Stellar job! Maybe I can accidentally launch some nukes as my crescendo.

I hear Bo knocking on my bedroom door and calling my name. Time to pay the piper, I guess. I was really hoping to get a few months under my belt before having to see this man mad.

I leave the bathroom and go to the bedroom door. I open it and cover my face with my hands.

"I am so sorry, Bo," I say. "I have these stupid noise-canceling earbuds, and I guess I lost track of time. That was so unprofessional of me, I don't know what my problem is. I guess I was caught up in the casual atmosphere here, and I just treated this place, your place, like it was my home, and that is unacceptable and…"

Bo shakes his head, "No, I'm sorry, Ellie. I should have let you know we were here. I knocked on the office door, and when I peeked in, I saw you were working out, so I decided not to interrupt you. Besides, Jasper should have locked the door leading to your office."

"So, that's Jasper, huh?" I say, still completely mortified. "I can't say that I have ever met another world leader in that exact way before. I guess I've made a strong first impression. I hope this doesn't complicate things for you too much. Should I go apologize?"

Bo laughs. "Really, don't worry about it. Jasper's not shy, clearly. This is probably the best time he has had in a while."

Looking at Bo, I smile. "Would you mind terribly if I board up the door leading to that bathroom?"

Bo laughs again and suddenly starts studying his feet. "Um, anyway," he says, "I will let you get back to it. I'm sure you want to shower and get dressed before dinner."

Looking down at myself, I realize that I am in nothing but a sports bra and boy shorts. Well, why not? If you are going to embarrass yourself, you might as well go all in.

"Oh shit," I say under my breath. To Bo, I say: "I swear, I'm not normally this unprofessional. I'm really not. I'm just going to go. I'll see you in like, a half hour for dinner. And please, please, tell Jasper how sorry I am."

"No problem," Bo says as he turns to leave. "See you at dinner."

※

Coming down the stairs, I can hear the two men talking in the kitchen. I guess they can hear me because they abruptly stop speaking. After a moment, they begin discussing which meals they would like to heat up for dinner.

I pause at the bottom of the stairs, gathering my courage to face Jasper. Maybe this time I'll see his face. I can feel my cheeks flushing with embarrassment again. Taking a deep breath, I march to the kitchen.

"Hello gentlemen," I say as I approach.

Bo and Jasper both face me. Jasper has a huge smile splitting his face. He is very handsome, with blond hair, crystal blue eyes, and bronze skin. He reminds me a little of Bo's advisor, Chester, except Jasper is built more like Bo. Maybe even a little bit broader in the shoulders. Wolfmen sure are big. I wonder if any of them ever considered playing professional sports.

Bo clears his throat and looks Jasper dead in the eyes. It seems a bit like a warning to me, which is odd, since Jasper is higher up the food chain than Bo. Strange.

"Jasper Adolpha, meet Eloise Margrave," Bo says. "Ellie, this is Jasper."

Summoning all of my courage, I look Jasper in the face, extend my hand to shake, and say: "Nice to officially meet you Mr. Adolpha."

Jasper laughs. "Please call me Jasper," he says, pulling me into a half-hug/half-handshake. And don't worry about earlier. The first look is always free, but the next one will cost you."

Jasper winks at me as I pull away a bit awkwardly. Bo looks like a disappointed father and then abruptly punches Jasper in the arm. My guess is that he asked Jasper to be on his best behavior, but Jasper would rather tease him.

All of us are standing incredibly close to each other now and it feels a bit weird to me, but the men don't seem to notice the strangeness of it.

Before I can move away and put some space between all of us, Bo nudges Jasper out of the way and shows me a bunch of dinner platters that he has laid out. "What would you like tonight, Ellie? We have steak, chicken, salmon, and meatloaf."

Looking back at the two men, I say, "I'll take the salmon if no one minds."

Neither man objects. They are still hovering very close to me, so as nicely as I can, I shoo them both to the other room while I heat up the platters.

"Why don't you two go catch up?" I say. "I'll get dinner ready and call you when it's done."

Jasper smiles and looks between me and Bo, "You better watch out, Ellie. If you keep taking care of him like this, Bo might never let you leave."

Bo just shakes his head and shoves Jasper out of the kitchen.

The two men head back toward Bo's office. I can hear Jasper teasing Bo, and I swear, I hear Bo growl.

Before I can ponder any of that, my phone dings. It's Janeal asking if I have met Jasper yet. I fill her in on my embarrassing first meeting, swearing her to secrecy. Based on all I know about her so far, the story might be on the front page of the local newspaper tomorrow.

The two of us talk while the meals are heating. She asks me to take stock of the remaining meals for her. She'll do some shopping and double them up now that Jasper is with us, too. Apparently, wolfmen eat a lot.

I call the two men back to the table, and we all sit down to eat together.

Jasper takes the seat across from me and says, "So, Ellie, Bo tells me that you are a globetrotter."

"Ich bin, ja," I respond. (Yes, I am.)

Jasper raises an eyebrow at me. "Sprichst du auch deutsch?" (You speak German too?)

Bo looks between the two of us.

Based on his expression, I am guessing he isn't strong in German. I decide that we had better switch back to English. "I speak enough to get by. I've lived all over the world, so I speak at least a little of all the major languages."

Jasper leans in, "Bo didn't tell me you were so extraordinary. Beautiful, smart, cultured. If you get tired of life in the States, you can most certainly come to stay with us in Germany. I think you would find it fascinating. We have an extensive library of historical texts dating back to the Vikings. Our pack is headquartered in Germany but includes the Netherlands, Denmark, Norway, and Sweden. We are the largest pack in the realm."

Bo glares at Jasper. "You can't have my ambassador, Jay."

I smile warmly, hoping to lighten Bo's mood. Jasper and Bo obviously have some sort of rivalry going on. It's pretty clear that Jasper is being overly complimentary to get a rise out of Bo. "I'm afraid Bo is right; I belong to the U.S. government, and my assignment is here. But I would love to visit your community sometime. It sounds amazing. I have so much to learn about your people."

Bo chimes in, "We are the second largest pack. Jasper never lets me forget it. But don't worry, we also have lots of material for you to study. We house duplicates of almost every text that Jasper has in his library."

"Yes," Jasper says, not taking his eyes off me. "But there is nothing like an original."

I get the idea that Jasper is trying to push Bo's buttons. This rivalry seems less political and more like siblings. The two look like they might be the same age, but as I learned earlier today, looks can be deceiving.

"How many people are in your pack?" I ask Jasper, hoping to change the subject and reel in this crazy train, at least a little bit.

It seems to work because Jasper has dropped the exaggerated smile and looks more like a normal person now. "We are just over one and a half million between the five countries. We have a large community town in Germany, with about 450,000 people, and another eight smaller towns with between 50,000 and 100,00 people each."

"Wow," I say. "So, even though you have more people overall, your headquarters city is actually smaller than Bo's. There are 600,000 living on this land, right?"

It's Bo's turn to smile widely.

"Why, yes," Bo says, rewarding me with a wink. "That is true. We support 600,000 within our headquarters borders. Which is also quite a bit larger, geographically speaking, than the German city. But I only have five small communities outside of our borders to contend with."

"OK, OK," Jasper says, holding his hands up in mock surrender. "I see how it is. Teaming up on me already. You win."

The rest of the dinner goes well. The three of us fall into comfortable conversation. I learn that Jasper and Bo have been friends since they were kids, which explains their sibling-like rivalry. Both attended a sort of boarding school for pack leaders. They require special education to understand pack law, Ulfheðnar customs and history, human customs and history, and to learn about the other realms.

"Wait," I say, putting down my fork. "There are more than two realms?"

Jasper drops his fork dramatically and leans back in his chair, crossing his arms. He looks at Bo with a frown. "Bo, haven't you taught our lovely friend here anything about the real world around her?"

Bo shakes his head at Jasper. "Come on, man, she's only known about us for a little over a week. I figured one thing at a time. I didn't want to fry her brain by dumping all of this on her at once."

Shaking his head, Jasper turns back to me. "Yes, there are more realms. There is a fae realm, a daemon realm, giants, and even vampires. Demons, giants, and vampires pretty much stay to themselves. But the fae love it here."

I am flabbergasted. "Are you serious?"

"Yeah," Jasper says, like he's just told me the most mundane thing ever, instead of the mind-shattering truth of faerie creatures walking amongst us.

"Do the fae look like us?" I ask. I am sure I look like a wide-eyed child, but at the moment, I don't care one bit.

"No, not really," Bo chimes in, his nose wrinkled in disgust. "They are usually at least 7.5 feet tall. Pointy ears and pasty white skin. All their teeth are pointed like human K9 teeth. Their hair is white, and their eyes are usually really pale too, almost no color."

I am still in shock. "Then how come they aren't noticed?"

This time, it is Jasper's turn to make a disgusted face. "The ugly fuckers use magic to conceal themselves. Most of your supermodels are fae men and women. They are masters of deceit and trickery. They have convinced the whole human world that their distorted human forms are the ideal beauty standard."

"That makes total sense," I say quietly. "No wonder girls are killing themselves trying to look like models. They literally can't. Does the human government know about this, too?"

Bo nods. "Yeah, they know. The fae have an agreement with the human governments just like we do. We trade services and they trade magic."

My eyebrows shoot up, "Magic?"

Jasper laughs at my naivety. "Yeah, magic. How else do you think the humans have come so far in such a short period of time? You really believe that cell phones work without magic? What's the official story…scientists shoot a satellite into space, that receives a transmission from your phone, then that satellite figures out what other phone you are trying to reach, finds that phone amongst the eight and a half billion other phones in the world, and beams your transmission to that phone, even when it is moving 160 km an hour in a train on the other side of the world, and it does all of that instantly."

My jaw drops open again. "Well, when you put it like that, it does sound a bit unbelievable."

Bo laughs. "The fae have only started interacting with humans in the last 200 years or so. Every time they push the boundaries too far and piss off the human authorities, they pay for peace by giving up a new form of magical tech."

My mind is racing. It explains so much, but still sounds insane at the same time.

Chapter Thirteen

Monday Morning, I head downstairs to find that Bo is already heating up his breakfast. I don't know if it is his size or because he is a wolf-man, but he sure eats a lot of food.

I make my own plate. There isn't much here to work with. Janeal meal preps for Bo, so he doesn't have a lot of unprepared foods. I do manage to find a couple of yogurt cups, one apple, and some canned peaches.

I take my place across from Bo and watch as he shovels food into his mouth. His face is twisted up in concentration, so I keep my greeting to a short 'good morning' and open my email on my phone.

After a few minutes, Bo suddenly burst out with a question about the most important part of a society. I wasn't really ready for a quiz this morning, and I wonder if he is trying to test me by ambushing me this early in the morning with such a heavy question.

Joke's on him, though. I was built for this.

Does he really think he is the first man to try to test my intelligence and prove to himself that I haven't earned my spot at the table? Metaphorically, of course, I don't think he's trying to kick me out of the dining room.

Although that would be funny.

I'm getting off-topic, stay focused. Society is a structure, and structures need solid foundations. Kids are the foundation of society. Bo prides himself on the equality of his people, I'm going to say, access to education.

"I think that the education system has always been a strong indicator of a community's overall strength," I say, as casually as I can muster. "If only the men or the rich or the powerful can access education, then what chance do the poor have to change their fate and make a better life for themselves?"

The corners of his mouth tick up just a little. I think I passed the test, but he is still trying to play it cool. That's right, buddy, not my first rodeo.

"Maybe I can take you on a tour of our school system after we're done eating," he says. "You can tell me how we stack up."

"Oh, you stack up fine," I blurt out before I can stop myself. "I just mean, you have equal opportunity here. There isn't really disparity amongst the people like in other parts of the world."

Way to ruin the upper hand there, Ellie. What is wrong with me? It's like he pushes the 'do something stupid' button in my brain.

Bo takes a bit too long to answer, but then he says, "I don't want to be just *fine*. I want to be the best you've ever seen."

Oh my. I pop a slice of apple into my mouth and try to keep my face neutral.

"Sure," I say, a bit too loudly. I guess that control over my features didn't extend to my voice.

Thankfully, Bo seems lost in thought again. He is shoveling the last bits of his massive breakfast into his face at a concerning pace. Is he trying to wrap this up quickly?

"Great," He finally says. "I'll get changed and meet you back here whenever you are ready."

"Just us," I ask. "Or is Jasper coming too?"

"His royal ass-ness likes to sleep in," he says, glancing toward the stairs. For a moment, I wonder if there is more to Jasper and Bo's relationship than friendship. Not that it's any of my business or anything.

I finish my plate and jog up the stairs. I don't want to keep Bo waiting, so I throw on the first thing I grab and twist my hair into a fake French twist I saw on the internet.

It is only a few minutes before I'm ready, and we head to the school.

The administration seems a little annoyed that we're here unplanned and unannounced. I can feel the anxiety curling in my gut. This is another test to see how I handle myself, I guess.

After a couple of calls to the different classrooms, we head to the auditorium where the kids will meet us. The staff are friendly, despite their obvious grievances about the surprise visit.

They tell me all about this school's students and how they divide the classrooms, grades, and districts.

This building houses students from Pre-K age to 3rd grade and then skips ahead to students from 10th grade to 12th grade.

Apparently, part of the curriculum for the older students is to help the younger students through their first years in school while they learn to shift and control their wolf form. Their last year in school focuses on community responsibility and civic duty instead of writing essays.

Students in 4th through 9th grade focus on academic studies in a separate building.

It's fascinating.

Bo mostly watches from the sidelines, and I catch him occasionally smirking. He takes great pride in his community and, from all I have seen so far, it's well earned.

Once the children enter the room, chaos descends. They rush me like I'm a celebrity or something. It is hard to make out any individual questions through the roar of excited child noises, but I do manage to answer a few.

From somewhere near the back of the crowd, I hear, "Miss Margrave, Miss Margrave, look what I can do!"

The adults and several of the older students yell at the boy to stop, but he is too focused on showing me his shift to hear them…or care.

Where there was once a chubby-faced second grader, there now stands a very excited wolf puppy.

Without warning, other children begin to shift into their wolf forms too. I know I should keep my composure right now, but honestly, who could resist a room full of wolf puppies?

Instinctively, I drop to the floor. So many puppies head straight for me. The fuzzy little ears and the wagging tails.

This is the best day of my life.

※

Bo and Jasper spend most of the afternoon in his office going over the case of the killer wolf man. The men seem content to handle the situation without me. Honestly, I don't think I'm ready for tracking killers of any kind, let alone supernatural beings.

Instead, I made plans for myself today.

First, I'm going into the city center to check out some of the home décor boutiques and get an idea of what I can buy locally and what I might need to order online for my new home.

Then, I want to go to the grocery store for some fresh produce. I prefer to eat fruit for breakfast in the morning. I also want to pick up some tea, which I like at night when I am unwinding.

Later, Roman and Francine invited me to their home for dinner.

Not wanting to interrupt Jasper and Bo in their meeting, I leave a note in the kitchen explaining my plans for the day and telling Bo to text me anything he needs.

When I climb into the SUV outside, I realize that I have no idea how to navigate the city. Luckily, once the car is started, I see the in-dash navigation system seems to have a custom map loaded for the Ulfsekir land.

Suddenly, I wonder if GPS is another example of fae magic-tech.

Best not to think too hard about it. I'll just give myself a headache.

I type the name of one of the stores I saw while I was out with Janeal yesterday, and start my drive into town. I drive slowly along the roads near Bo's house. There are so many animals in the woods, and I am completely unfamiliar with the area.

I notice a car behind me, so I pull over and wave them past. Instead of going around, the driver stops and rolls down the window.

I do the same and smile down at the man in the sedan anxiously.

He leans across his center console and yells, "Hello there. Is everything OK?"

I smile at the gesture. I really thought this would be a road rage incident and that I would be getting cursed out for driving so slow on these back roads.

"Everything is fine, sir," I say. "I'm sorry to hold you up. I'm just new around here and I'm not too sure about the roads yet. Figured I better go slow, better safe than sorry, ya know."

"Ah, OK," he says. "You must be the human ambassador. I won't hold you up then. Welcome to the pack and have a great day!"

"Thank you so much," I say. "You, too, have a great day."

With that, we both put up our windows, and he drives off ahead of me. It's going to take a while for me to get used to how nice and genuinely helpful everyone is here. I definitely don't hate it.

Bo told me before we traveled here that being helpful and supporting other pack members was a point of pride among his people, but I didn't really understand it until I got here. That man didn't have to stop and check on me. He could have been mad that I was holding him up, or he could have just driven right past me. The fact that he stopped just to make sure I was OK gave me the warm and fuzzies inside.

Hell, if he had just driven by and waved at me, I would have thought he was a nice man. Instead, he stopped and asked if I was OK. Then wished me a good day and welcomed me to his hometown. It's such a culture shock, and honestly, it shouldn't be. I hadn't even realized how much anxiety we carry around with us in the human world. We live in constant fear of confrontation with others.

With a start, I realize that I have been mindlessly driving along, lost in my thoughts, and I'm already at the strip mall parking garage.

I leave the SUV behind and head to the first store on my list. Inside, I am greeted by a woman who looks to be around my age, though she could be much older than I think.

The woman introduces herself as Ember. It's a beautiful name, and I tell her how much I like it.

She smiles and thanks me. "You are the new human in town, right?"

"I am," I say to her. "Am I that obvious?"

She laughs and shakes her head, "It's nothing you are doing, it's just your scent. Wolves have a slight musk. Without that, it's pretty easy to deduce that you're the human everyone is talking about."

"Ah, yes," I say, nodding my head. "I am learning that scent is a very big deal. I can barely tell one flower from another, let alone identify a person."

"Rumor has it that you are living with Bo," she says in a clearly forced, casual manner.

"I'm not really living with him," I say. "I'm just staying in his guest room while my new house is being finished. That's actually why I'm here. I wanted to start looking for furniture and stuff."

Ember looks a little relieved to hear me say that I'll be leaving Bo's house soon. If I had to guess, she is either an ex-girlfriend or a wannabe girlfriend. Either way, she has a vested interest in Bo, and I am not here for any love triangle drama.

We wander around the store, and Ember asks me about my style, asking me to rate different items so that she can get a feel for what I like. I explain to her that I spent most of my life traveling, and this is my first home. She seems aghast at the very idea of never having a home, but she keeps it very professional.

We look at so many different things, and she asks my opinion about each item. It seems that I fall into what Ember calls contemporary minimalist style. According to her, identifying my style will help me narrow down my choices and keep me from getting overwhelmed by options. She is quite good at her job.

During our time together, Ember peppers our conversation with questions about Bo and our relationship. She is especially curious to know if Bo has mentioned anyone in particular within the pack.

I explain to her, in as many ways as I can think of, that we are just professional colleagues and barely friends. I hardly know anything about his personal life, aside from the fact that he and Jasper are friends.

She still seems disappointed that he didn't somehow bring her up to me.

I get it. She obviously has some sort of feelings for Bo, but what did she expect? "Hi, I'm Bo, and I know a girl named Ember who works at a home decor store in a town that you've never heard of."

I never understood the way people act when they have a crush on someone. I just don't have time for that sort of thing. Even as a young girl, I couldn't be bothered. Maybe it's because we never stuck around any one place long enough for me to really become attached to anyone. I'm sure a therapist would have a field day pulling on that thread.

I end up buying a few things from Ember and promise to come back for more when the house is ready. Despite her not-so-subtle hints at a relationship with Bo, I like her. She was very nice and extremely helpful. I'm sure that with her guidance, my new home will look amazing.

My next stop is the grocery store. I find myself avoiding the aisles with people in them. I really just want to get in and out. My social battery is nearly exhausted from Ember, and I still have to get through a dinner at Roman and Francine's tonight.

Luckily, the grocery store employees are much less chatty, but still very friendly, and I am out of there with my produce and tea in no time. Since the pack provides staple foods for free, and the produce is mostly local, I barely pay anything at the checkout.

When I get back to the house, Bo and Jasper are in Bo's conference room. It sounds like they are both on separate calls with different people.

I bring my groceries to the kitchen, put the refrigerated items away, and put the tea in the cabinet with the coffee. There isn't a space for the bananas, apples, and oranges, but I have a plan. I bought a nice plain silver fruit dish from Ember today. I'll just use that while I am here.

I arrange the fruit, then head upstairs to get ready for dinner at Roman's.

※

Pulling up to Roman and Francine's house, I notice extra cars around the driveway. I guess our quiet dinner will have a few more people than I planned for.

Before I can even knock, Candy opens the door and immediately pulls me in for a strong hug. You would have thought I was her long-lost daughter returned to her at last.

"I'm so happy to see you," Candy says, ushering me into the house. "Come, come, there are some people I would like you to meet."

Candy leads me into the family room, and I see Roman, Francine, and two other people I haven't met yet, a man and a woman. The woman is just as striking as Candy. She has very similar features and that same long, thick, dark hair.

The man looks very familiar, too.

"Ellie Margrave, this is my sister Jasmine and her husband Gorm Ragnulf," Candy says, very excitedly.

Oh. Shit. Balls.

These are Bo's parents. That is why the man looks so familiar. I see it clear as day now, he is an older version of Bo.

I shake hands with Jasmine, and when I shake hands with Grom, he apologizes and gives me his left hand. "I injured my right paw six years ago in a poacher's trap. Crushed the bones, and now my human hand doesn't squeeze so well."

We talk back and forth a bit about poachers and how they sometimes hear stories about big wolves in the area and try to catch one for skinning. Grom says the injury doesn't bother him too much, but he does have a hard time with doorknobs.

A thought clicks into place in my mind. Bo doesn't have a single doorknob in his house. Every single one of them is lever style. I smile internally as the understanding dawns on me. Bo doesn't want his father to have a hard time opening doors in his house.

Turning my attention to Candy, I say, "So, Bo is your nephew? That's so nice that you two get to work together. You guys must have a very tight-knit family."

Francine pokes her head into the room and announces that dinner is ready. Candy threads her arm through mine and we head to the dining room.

Just as we are all getting ready to sit, Roman, Candy, and I each get a message from Bo.

We all look at our phones, and I frown a bit. Bo's mother, Jasmine, asks us what is wrong.

I say, "Apparently, Jasper and Bo have a lead on where this man they're tracking is. It looks like they are flying out tonight to Cedar Crest, New Mexico, and will check in with us when they have more information."

Candy and Roman look at each other, then at me with bewilderment in their eyes.

Roman speaks first. "You got all that, huh?"

Candy laughs softly, and I'm suddenly confused. She adds, "Our message says: Following a lead. Taking Jasper's jet. Call tomorrow."

I smile awkwardly. I guess Bo didn't want me to worry when I returned to the house and they were gone. "Oh. Well, he knows that I'm here with you, he probably didn't want to type it out all over again and figured I would fill you in."

"Sure," Candy says as we take our seats. "That's probably exactly why he typed out a full explanation to you and sent Roman and me barely enough words to form complete thoughts."

"Anyway," Jasmine says, thankfully changing the subject. "Tell us about yourself, Ellie. Roman and Candy are both absolutely smitten with you, and Francine, Grom, and I have just been dying to meet you in person. We don't talk to many humans, for obvious reasons."

PART TWO:

BO

Chapter Fourteen

From my room, I hear Ellie let out a shrieking scream. I run down the hall, look in her office, and see the bathroom door open. I swing open the hall entrance to the bathroom just in time to see Jasper's towel fall to the ground while he is holding his hands up in the air.

"What the hell is going on?" I yelled at him. "Pick up your fucking towel."

Did Ellie just check him out? She is still staring.

Jasper is just laughing. At least Ellie has finally turned away from his naked body.

"Are you kidding me, Jay?" I'm still kind of yelling. "You've been here 5 minutes and you're already flashing your dick at my ambassador."

Suddenly, Ellie starts yelling, "I'm so sorry. I had my earbuds in, and I lost track of time, and I was sweaty, and I didn't know anyone was here. Oh my God, I'm so sorry. I'm so embarrassed. I'm going to go to my room now and die of shame. Bye."

She slams the door behind her, and I can hear her run into her room and then her bathroom.

I give Jasper a warning look and say, "Not cool, man."

I turn and walk out of the bathroom, then knock on Ellie's door to make sure she is OK.

She answers the door in her tiny little yoga outfit. She was stunning in her evening gown, and obviously in great shape, but I had no idea yoga could make you look like that. I apologize to her for not letting her know that we were in the house, and when I catch myself gawking at her, I quickly look down and excuse myself.

It never occurred to me that Ellie would just go from her office to the adjacent bathroom after her yoga sessions. I had no idea that yoga made you sweat like that. I swear to Luna that I'll strangle Jasper if he did that on purpose.

I'm going to have to adjust to having a woman in my house. Jasper is damn well going to adjust too.

I head downstairs and grab a beer. A few minutes later, Jasper comes down, freshly showered and with a huge grin on his smug-ass face.

He leans into me, "Damn, man, that Ellie has a hella tight body, huh. Are you sure she doesn't have a little wolf in her?"

I am already shaking my head. I know what his next words are going to be.

"Cause I'd put some in her," he says.

I shove him, fairly hard, in the shoulder. "That is my ambassador, Jay. Remember the treaty that says that wolves can't have relationships with humans? The one that she is here to uphold."

"So, what?" Jasper says. "Not like we haven't banged humans before."

I can feel my anger rising. "This isn't some barista, at a random coffee shop. That is my U.S. ambassador. Her job is to uphold treaties and our says no humans. Plus, the humans we have been with don't know what we are; they think we are human. This is totally different, and you know it."

"I don't know," Jasper says, with a smirk. This asshole is playing with me. "I think she liked what she saw."

Jasper and I stop talking when we hear Ellie's footsteps approaching.

Jasper is my best friend, the closest thing I have to a brother. It'll be a damn shame if he makes me punch him in that pretty face tonight.

※

"What do you think the most important part of a social system is?" I ask out of the blue.

Ellie's face tilts up from her plate of fruit and some kind of creamy thing, maybe yogurt or something. Ok, maybe that was a weird question, especially for first thing in the morning. I spent the last five minutes trying to think of an impressive conversation starter. I thought I nailed it, but her face says otherwise. Shit.

"I think that the education system has always been a strong indicator of a community's overall strength," Ellie finally replies. "If only the men or the rich or the powerful can access education, then what chance do the poor have to change their fate and make a better life for themselves?"

I take it back; that was a great question. I did nail it.

"Maybe I can take you on a tour of our school system after we're done eating," I say with a bit more confidence behind my tone. "You can tell me how we stack up."

"Oh, you stack up fine," she says. I can see the blush creeping into her cheeks as she hurries on. "I just mean, you have equal opportunity here. There isn't really disparity amongst the people like in other parts of the world."

I like that I made her blush a little. She sure as hell knocks me off of my game, so it's only fair.

OK, witty come back, witty come back.

"I don't want to be just *fine*," I say, letting my voice drop and my bass resonate. "I want to be the best you've ever seen."

The pink is back in her cheeks. Yes! I don't know why I am so exhilarated by the sight of my ambassador blushing. We are strictly professional.

She's human. She's a government official.

It must be my hunter instincts. She's a new, eligible, beautiful, intelligent woman. And with Jasper here now, another man in my domain, of course, my natural instincts will want her to like me best. It doesn't mean anything; it's just the wolf side of me. The walker side of me knows that it's just harmless, playful, light flirting.

"Sure," Ellie replies. Jolting me from my thoughts and reminding me that I had asked her a question.

"Great," I say, finishing up my plate of waffles, eggs, and sausage. "I'll get changed and meet you back here whenever you are ready."

"Just us," Ellie asks. "Or is Jasper coming too?"

"His royal ass-ness likes to sleep in," I say with a smirk.

I grab myself a blue button-down, then put it back and grab a white one. I put that one back, too. This time, I grab a green one. I've been told that green is a good color for me. Candy and Janeal both say that it brings out my skin's olive undertones.

Whatever that means.

Ellie meets me downstairs a few minutes later. She's wearing a cream-colored shirt and dark blue dress pants. She looks great, classy, and like the kind of woman who commands respect when she walks into a room. She looks like a real leader.

※

Our tour of the school creates chaos. All the children scramble to see the human in town. Some of them want to meet me, too, but mostly they're curious about Ellie.

I get more than a few stern looks from the school's teachers and administrators. It's a good thing I'm their boss.

Ellie is great with inquisitive little ones. The younger kids fight for her attention by jumping and squealing, while the older kids ask rapid-fire questions about life in the human world.

126

I take a step forward to intervene, but the smile on her face and the light in her eyes is enough to keep me at bay.

"Miss Margrave, Miss Margrave," a little boy toward the back of the crowd yells. "Look what I can do!"

Two teachers and an aide yell, "NO," but they are too late. The boy, about 8 if I had to guess, starts to shift into a tiny wolf pup. The shift of one child sets off a chain reaction across the room, and before long, there are more than a dozen pups yapping and nipping at each other.

Not all the kids can shift yet, and the older students have better control, so at least some of the children have remained in their human forms.

The stern looks from the staff are a lot closer to sneers now. Oops.

Ellie drops to the floor, and every single pup heads straight for her.

The yips and sharp barks mix with the joyful laughter flowing out of Ellie, and it creates a symphony unlike anything I have ever heard in my life.

It takes the staff takes a solid 20 minutes to get the children back under control, and I help out as much as I can. I'll be hearing about this later, for sure.

We duck out of the side exit and leave the kids in the hands of the professionals. Ellie is still glowing with delight when she climbs into the SUV.

"That was amazing," she says as I hop into the driver's seat. "I don't know what I expected, but that was awesome. I mean, obviously, werewolf kids would turn into little wolf puppies, but holy shit that was the cutest thing I've ever seen."

Chapter Fifteen

Jasper and I have been in the office and conference room all day calling police stations, ranger stations, newspapers, and hospitals to follow up on any suspicious animal attacks.

The guy we are hunting must be a complete sociopath. Our theory is that he befriends women, sometimes dates them, showers them with love and affection, and then lures them into the woods and kills them. But we have no idea why.

We know he is a strong wolf. Jasper believes that he is only partially shifting when he tortures these women. There is a mixture of injuries on them, both hand-made and claw marks, but usually no bites. We think that he terrifies them by turning into a half-beast before attacking them.

He isn't shy about the killings either, and several police forces around the globe are looking for him. Of course, they are looking for a human man who doesn't really exist in their world.

The same protocols that we use to keep our people safe are now allowing this man to dodge us and travel freely. All he needs to do is show up in any wolf community and ask for a human identity, and he can recreate himself as often as he needs to.

The only things we have to go on are the medical examiner reports and vaguely similar composite sketches. It's not a lot, but this isn't our first time tracking a rogue wolf.

We get lucky when we hear back from a community contact who tells us that he gave a new human identity to a man matching our description. The name is Roberto Garcia, and the state of issue is New Mexico.

"Let's make some calls after we eat. We'll concentrate on that area," I say. "There have got to be thousands of Roberto Garcias in that region. Maybe we'll get lucky and find a wolf who scented someone new in town."

Jasper and I walk out to the kitchen and find a fruit display on my kitchen island. Next to it is a note from Ellie in neat handwriting:

> I'm running into the city to do some browsing and pick up some fruit and tea. I'll be stopping home then heading to Roman & Francine's for dinner. Call or text if you need anything.
>
> -Ellie
>
> I met Ember. she says "Hi."
>
> Hope you don't mind the fruit bowl. I didn't know where else to put it. ☺

Jasper looks over my shoulder to read the note.

"This is how it starts, man," he says, pointing to the fruit bowl. "Today it's a fruit bowl, tomorrow it's new curtains, next thing you know, you have fancy dishes that you're only allowed to use when company comes over."

I'm only half listening to him. Ellie wrote "home" in her note. I'm not really sure why, but it makes me feel incredibly satisfied inside that she referred to my house as home.

"Who the hell is Ember," Jasper asks as he bites into a cold chicken breast straight out of a meal container.

How did human men trick their women into thinking that men are the providers? Without Janeal to prepare my meals, Jasper and I would be trying to fuel ourselves with chips and salsa, and maybe some sort of snack cake.

"Ugh," I say. "She's a girl that Chester's girlfriend tried to set me up with. She introduced Ember to my mother, who then insisted that I give her a chance. I talked to her a few times, and she's nice, but I blew her off for my trip to D.C. I guess she mentioned that to Ellie today."

"Awe, shit," Jasper says in a teasing tone. "Girl fight."

"Jay," I say, putting the note back on the counter. "You are my oldest friend, my brother from another mother. Please don't make me kill you. My mom will be so pissed at me if I kill you. She loves you."

Jasper puffs up his chest and smiles, chicken hanging out of the corner of his mouth. "I am her favorite."

"You'll probably be losing that title to Ellie tonight," I say with a wicked grin. "She's having dinner at Roman's house, it's Sunday night, so Mom, Dad, and Aunt Candy will be there."

Jasper lets his jaw drop mockingly. "You're letting her meet your parents without you? Are you sure you don't want to head over there right now? We can pick this up again tomorrow. I'll come too; I want to see this."

I raise my eyebrows at him, "Why would I do that? Ellie knows Roman and Candy pretty well, and she's a born ambassador. Surprising her with our former pack leaders isn't going to knock her off her game."

Jasper shakes his head, "I'm not talking about our former pack leaders, stupid. I'm talking about your new HUMAN girlfriend meeting your parents for the first time without you. Specifically, your human-fearing mother."

"She's not my girlfriend," I say before I can stop myself. I know what he is doing. This is a trap. He is baiting me into a discussion about Ellie, where no matter what I say, it'll lead to him backing me into a corner. I don't want to play this game with him. I take a breath.

"You're being childish," I say.

"OK," Jasper says. "If you say so, Mr. She's Not My Girlfriend."

"She's my ambassador," I say.

Jasper puts up his hands and laughs. "Yeah, I know. You've told me like 20 times. Are you reminding me, or are you reminding yourself? Since when do we give a fuck about the human's rules anyway? Ellie seems amazing, and I'm telling you now, man, if you don't lock that down, someone else is going to. Shit, I might take a run at it."

I stand up to my full height and step closer to Jasper.

Again, this asshole laughs in my face. Laughs. He says, "Told you, bro. You're 2 seconds from challenging me because I said that I *might* try to seduce your *NOT* girlfriend."

I shrink back down and lean against the kitchen island again.

Jasper softens his tone, "Just admit to yourself that you like her. You don't have to admit it to me because I already know."

My phone dings.

"It's the guy that gave Roberto his ID," I say to Jasper. "He looked back at the paperwork and saw that he gave the guy a prepaid credit card with a few hundred dollars on it. Turns out, he used it at a hotel in Cedar Crest."

Jasper perks up. "Hell yeah, I'll call the airfield, let's get down there. Don't forget to drop a line to your honey boo boo."

I swear to Luna, I am going to kill him and throw his body out of his own damn jet.

"You're an asshole, Jay," I yell to him as he heads back to the office to grab his phone.

While he's gone, I text Ellie to let her know what's going on. I also message Roman, Chester, and Candy in our group chat.

I feel terrible leaving her alone after she just got here.

After a moment, I text Janeal and ask her to keep an eye on Ellie for me.

Janeal sends me back: "Don't worry boss, I'll make sure the boys behave around her."

What the fuck does that mean? Are men already approaching Ellie? She's only been here for 2 days.

Maybe I should give her a bullet-point overview of the treaty. She should know about the relationship amendment, sooner rather than later. Not that I care if she dates someone. I just want to make sure she knows about the treaty rules, since she takes her job so seriously.

Chapter Sixteen

The flight to Albuquerque won't take very long, especially on Jasper's plane.

The pilot tells us that we're cleared to land in about 3 hours, so we'll be taking off soon. Without anything else to do before we leave, I take out my phone and text Ellie.

How's dinner with Aunt Candy and my parents?

You knew they were coming to dinner?????

They have dinner with Roman and Francine every Sunday.

Oh, you could have told me.
Also…Candy is your mom's sister?

I told you that we are a close family community.

Anything else I should know?

I think Jasper has a crush on you.

Duh, why else would he flash me on the first date!

Jasper is heading toward me to take his seat. I had better wrap this up before he gets the wrong idea.

Plane is taking off, I'll check in later.

Ok, please be safe.

I look up to meet Jasper's gaze. Fuck. I must have been making a face. Jasper is ear-to-ear grinning at me.

"What?" I say in my most annoyed tone.

"Checking in with Miss Not My Girlfriend?" He says in a child-like voice as he throws an arm around my shoulder.

I hit him with a tiny airplane pillow as hard as I can. "I told you," I say, "I *will* kill you and live with my mother's disappointment. I was just making sure she made out ok with Mom and Dad. You're the one who thought it was wrong to send her in unprepared."

"Yeah, sure." Jasper isn't having any of my nonsense. "I don't understand why you don't just admit that you like her. I'm not asking you to propose to her and pop out little halfling babies. But you clearly like her."

"It doesn't matter," I say. "Even if I did like her, I can't do anything about it. She is my ambassador."

Jasper looks me straight in the eyes and says, "I swear to Luna, if you say 'she's my ambassador' one more time, I'll punch you in the fucking throat."

"I'm only saying it because you seem to forget that it's a big deal," I say. "I can't cross any lines with her."

"That's bullshit," Jasper says, dropping into a seat next to me. "No one cares about a one-line amendment to a 100-year-old treaty."

"Ellie does," I say. "Besides, that amendment was put in there for a reason."

Jasper shakes his head, "Yeah, to keep love-sick puppies from spilling all our secrets to every pretty face they see. Ellie already knows about us. You wouldn't be betraying the spirit of the amendment. Yeah, buddy, I'm a politician too, remember."

Oh, shit. I hate it when he's all political know-it-all. Mainly because he's usually right.

"Even if," I say, "and it's a big if, even if I did like her. So, what, it can't go anywhere? I'm an alpha and she's a human. She's gonna die more than hundred years before me, we can't produce the next generation of alpha, or worse, we have a terrible relationship, and we still have to work with each other for the next 40 years."

Jasper is clearly exasperated with me. "You think too much, my man. This is why you can't find love. You are always focused on the ending when you should be enjoying the present moment."

"OK," I say, "If you have it so figured out, then what's your excuse for being single?"

Jasper scrunches his face at me, "What do you mean? I'm single because I want to be single. I'm not ready to settle down and start a family. I won't even start thinking about that until I'm 60. But you are not me. I'm a whore, you're a family man."

I shake my head and roll my eyes at him. I don't understand why Jasper is suddenly so interested in my love life. It's like my mother paid him off to get grandpups.

"Why do you even care?" I say. "You've never pushed me towards a woman before. You don't even really know Ellie, you spent one dinner talking to her."

"You still don't get it, man." He says, sitting back in his seat. "I don't have to know her at all, because I do know you. I don't have to talk to her, all I have to do is see you talk to her. You look different when she's in the room. You smile when you look at your phone, and you want to rip my throat out when I talk about her. I've never seen any of that before. You even smell better."

"If you say so," is my only comeback. Weak, but it's all I've got.

"You're my brother," he says, reclining his chair to get comfortable. "I'm not going to sit back and watch you talk yourself out of something special. For what? There isn't anything that we can't figure out. You can't be the first human lover in the history of alphas."

"I'm not a human lover," I say. We're right back to children again. "Besides, don't we have a rogue killer to catch or something? There are much more pressing things to deal with than my non-love life."

Jasper closes his eyes and kicks off his shoes, "Whatever you say, boss."

※

Hopping into our rental car, Jasper types the name of Roberto's hotel into his phone's GPS. We are only about a half-hour drive from the last place that we know this guy, Roberto, has been.

Neither of us talks much on the drive. We're both amped up for a fight with a crazy killer wolf, and honestly, I'm still kind of annoyed with Jasper.

This new obsession of his with me and Ellie is getting on my nerves. How does he just live his life like an impulsive child with our entire race of people relying on him? I'm not just another wolf in the pack; I'm the alpha, and I have a responsibility to my people. I need to keep our pack strong.

My bloodline is among the purest of Ulfheðnar hybrids. Dad used to joke that with only a percent more, we wouldn't be able to shift into humans. I can't take that away from my pack because I have a crush on a human.

It's not even a crush. She's just new and exciting. It'll wear off after a little while, and everything will be fine. I'm only paying extra attention to her because she is new to this world, and I want to make sure we make a good first impression.

I need her to fight hard for us when it counts. The only way to make sure that she fights for us the way we need her to is to make sure she feels like she's one of us. Which means that I have to be attentive and make sure that she's comfortable.

There is nothing wrong with that. It doesn't mean anything. I am just doing what I need to do.

"What's going on over there?" Jasper says, jolting me back to reality.

For a moment I think he means inside of my head, but then I notice the commotion on the side of the road ahead of us. Off to the right,

I can see police cars, two ambulances, and a crowd of people gathered around some nearby trees.

"Think that could be our guy?" I say. "Do you wanna stop or keep heading to the hotel?"

"Let's head to the hotel," Jasper says. "Even if it is our guy, he isn't going to be in there now. Maybe we'll get lucky, and he'll head back to the hotel to clean up before he moves on. Either way, I'd rather avoid the local P.D. if we can."

I drive past the commotion and continue toward the hotel, it's only another 10 minutes ahead, according to the GPS. We need to stay focused on catching this guy, so I push all thoughts of Ellie out of my head. He's already killed at least 5 humans that we know of.

Of course, there could be many more that we don't know of. We are relying on human authorities to determine the causes of death, and they have no idea what to look for with a rogue wolf. That is, if they even find a body.

Since this guy is taking his victims into the woods, they could go weeks or months before they are found, and then, the police might file it as an accident or an unknown cause of death. There would be no way for us to tie those deaths to our guy.

"There it is," Jasper says, pointing to the tiny motel & RV park's entrance.

The parking lot is mostly dirt, with a sprinkling of those sharp grey rocks, and the office is nothing more than a shed. So much for sneaking up on this guy. We are totally exposed, and if he is out here, he might scent us before we can even get close.

The RV park motel backs up to the same woods where we saw the commotion down the road, which doesn't bode well for us.

We walk up to the shed office and find a kid of about 16 playing on a cell phone. Without looking away from his phone, he asks, "Ya need a lot or cabin?"

"Neither," I say. "We are looking for a friend of ours. Kinda big. Dark blonde hair. Weird accent for a guy named Roberto Garcia. Ring a bell?"

The kid still doesn't put down the phone. "Yeah, that dude's in the far cabin. Number 62 all the way in the back. Can't miss it."

Jasper and I don't waste any time. He goes left and I go right. We make our way to the back of the park on foot, so we don't draw any unwanted attention. Right now, the only advantage we have is that this guy doesn't yet know that we are looking for him.

He is only trying to evade the human police, and that's easy when you can shift into an animal to get away.

We cover the ground between the office and the back of the park in seconds. We move with our wolf speed and stealth. As alpha wolves, Jasper and I can both call on our wolves' strength and speed when needed.

Having the grace and agility of a predator can really help you sneak up on people. Especially in this type of terrain. The road to the back of the RV park isn't paved so we are moving over rocks and dirt.

When we can see the cabin, we stop and take cover. Our enhanced hearing means that we are able to whisper to each other even though we are at least 100 feet apart.

"Do you see any movement?" I ask.

Jasper just shakes his head, no.

We advance again. Now we are just outside the cabin on either side. Now, we can both hear movement inside.

There is only one door to the cabin. With a nod, we both approach the door and I try the knob. The door swings open, and Jasper and I both use our bodies to block the opening.

Inside the tiny cabin, we find Roberto in his wolf form. His fur is matted with blood. To the right is a small cot, and on it there is a badly mutilated human body. Without warning, the wolf charges at us. Jasper and I grab for him and loop our arms around his body.

The wolf is strong, and he flails and wiggles his massive frame in our grip. The blood makes his fur so slippery.

It takes all our strength and speed to keep his back legs from gutting one of us as he kicks furiously to escape our hold. His head is swinging wildly from side to side while he desperately tries to bite us.

The scuffle draws the attention of some campers staying nearby. At least three humans are watching us fight this giant wolf now.

There is no way we can shift in front of them to fight Roberto wolf-on-wolf. The blood in his fur is making it impossible to hold on to him. Sensing that he is gaining the upper hand, he stops trying to bite us and puts all his effort into getting out of our grip.

It doesn't take long before he slips us and heads straight for the human spectators. The people all scream and run desperately for the nearest RV.

Jasper immediately takes off toward Roberto, and I aim for the humans.

Jasper is able to lunge forward and grab the wolf's tail. It slows him down enough for me to get past him and place myself between him and the human campers.

Roberto throws his head back toward his tail with lightning speed and snaps his jaws at Jasper's hand. Jasper releases and pulls his hand back with only millimeters to spare. But now Jasper is on his back on the ground, and Roberto is heading straight for his throat.

Jasper is fast, but I know he can't get out of the way quickly enough. I do the only thing I can and throw my whole body at the wolf's back. I hop on top of him and wrap my arms and legs around his body as best I can. In my human form, I'm about 225lbs, so my surprise weight easily takes the wolf to the ground.

We tumble together, and I struggle to keep my chest tight against Roberto's back. If he gets even an inch of space, he'll turn and rip my throat out.

The blood from Roberto's fur coats my whole body, and I can't keep my grip tight enough around him. I'm thrown off his back and hit the ground with a sickening thud that knocks the wind right out of me. Thankfully, Jasper is back on his feet and storming towards us as I fight to keep Roberto's jaws from sinking into my flesh.

More humans are starting to appear, and the danger is increasing with every single second that slides by. If Roberto decides to go after these stupid, curious humans, we'll never get the upper hand.

With Jasper closing the gap between us, Roberto jumps off of me and directs his attention towards Jasper. I quickly roll to a crouching position, ready to throw my body between him and the approaching humans, who seem oblivious to the threat. Roberto stares us down with white-hot anger in his eyes. The fur from his head to the middle of his back is standing straight up in blood-clotted spikes.

For a moment, we all stare at each other, waiting for the next move. Roberto stares straight into our eyes; not an ounce of fear or submission to be seen in his gaze.

In the distance, sirens blare from a rapidly approaching police car. I can see it in his eyes, Roberto knows that he's beaten, for now.

Growling and baring his fangs, the wolf leaps over Jasper and takes off at full speed into the woods.

Jasper and I both turn to run after him when we hear the police officers yelling for us to freeze.

FUCK!

Chapter Seventeen

"Sorry about detaining you boys like this," the officer says to us. "But to be honest, when I saw the size of you fellas and all that blood, I wasn't takin' any chances."

The police immediately handcuffed Jasper and me when they arrived. I can't blame them. It was a wild scene and an even wilder story.

Luckily, the humans we saved were eager to tell the police how the two strangers fist-fought a giant wolf. We told the police that we were looking for our friend and found the wolf in his cabin.

"You boys are either the bravest or the craziest sons-a-bitches I ever met in my life," the officer continues. "I sure am glad you're on our side. That rabid wolf already killed two people, and if not for you boys, probably would have taken a few more before the day was out."

"Two people?" Jasper says, faking a surprised tone for the cops.

"Yuppers," the old officer continues. "There was a young lady found in the woods near that RV park you fellas were at. That's how we got to y'all so quick, we were only down the road a bit, there."

We are happy to let the officers believe whatever they want, as long as it isn't the truth. Of course, in a small town like this, they aren't looking too hard into a case like this one. They don't question things like, how did the wolf open the door to the cabin to get inside? Where did a giant wolf come from around here? Why go into a cabin and skip over the people already outside or in simple tents?

They're just happy to say the case is closed and move on. They would rather believe anything but murder by shape shape-shifting psycho.

Jasper and I play along. We've been down this road before. We talk to the officers about how crazy adrenaline is and how we can't believe we just did that. Blah, blah, blah.

If the cops hadn't been so close when the fight broke out, we would have been able to run after Roberto into the woods, we could have shifted once we were out of eyeshot. That asshole should have been dead by now.

Jasper and I are strong as humans, even stronger as wolves, and unstoppable together. We have been fighting together for 40 years. We don't need to talk; we know our roles, and we guard each other's backs. There isn't a force in this realm that can handle the two of us together. It made for a very interesting high school and college experience for us.

The cops and a couple of humans from the RV park spend a few minutes praising us and shaking our hands before one of them finally offers to drive us back to our car. Once we get there, we waste no time leaving.

We need to get checked into our hotel to regroup and shower.

Jasper loads up the map on his phone, and we head back the way we came.

"What the fuck was that?" I say, once we are back on the road.

"No shit," Jasper responds. "Our old friend Roberto is one hell of a wolf. Why are the crazy ones always so big?"

"Right," I say with a snorted laugh. "He's got to be from an alpha line. There's no way he's that strong and that big without some thick blood. Plus, did you see how he stared us both down? No one has been able to stare us in the eye like that since 5th grade."

Jasper shakes his head. "I don't know who this guy could be. I would hope that any of the other packs would let us know if they lost a bloodthirsty alpha."

"Me too," I add. "But that guy was strong. Strong like us, and we're the strongest wolves that we know of. So where did this guy come from?"

"You make a great point," Jasper agrees. "If any of the other packs had a thick-blooded alpha like that, we would have seen him before now. And I've definitely never met that wolf. He doesn't smell familiar at all."

I take a minute to think through everything we know.

"We've been working on the assumption that this started in your pack," I say to Jasper, "but what if it started in Iceland?"

"OK," Jasper says. "I'm listening. What makes you think that?"

"We told the kid at the office that Roberto had a funny accent because we assumed he was German," I say. "We asked the community ID handler if he had a German accent, but he could have mistaken his accent for German when it was really Icelandic."

"OK," Jasper says, "but what led you to Iceland?"

"Think about it," I say. "If this guy was in your pack, I don't care how many you have, you would have noticed him. If he were in the African or Asian packs, he would have stuck out like a sore thumb and definitely taken on their alphas by now. That leaves my remote Canadian regions and Iceland."

"OK," Jasper says. "I'm following you so far."

"Well," I say. "If he were in Canada, why go to all the way to Germany and then return back to the U.S.? We think he left Germany because you were chasing him, right?"

Jasper nods his head. "Motherfucker. That makes sense. If he were in Canada, completely undetected, why come to Germany only to come back to North America? In Iceland, he could go pretty unnoticed, even as a big alpha. They are almost all alphas there. As long as he didn't cause too much fuss, they wouldn't even think twice about him. Fucking Iceland."

We drive the rest of the way to our hotel in silence. Dealing with the Iceland pack is always a hassle, and that's without accusing them of unleashing a lunatic on the world. They're gonna love this.

※

After I shower, I finally pick up my phone to look up my Iceland pack contact numbers.

Before I can make any calls, I see texts from my mother, Roman, Candy, Chester, Ember, Janeal, and Ellie.

I open Ellie's first, but only because I want to make sure everything is OK while I am gone.

> *I hope everything is going ok for you. Don't worry about anything here, your parents are really sweet. Be safe, good night.*

I look at the clock, 10 p.m. Not too bad. Type back a quick reply.

> *I wouldn't say it went good, but Jasper and I are still in one piece.*
> *I'll call tomorrow and fill you in.*
> *Sleep well, good night.*

I move on to the group chat with Chester, Candy, and Roman

> *Met our mystery wolf. Didn't get him but didn't die either.*
>
> *I'll fill you all in tomorrow.*

Next, I open the message from my mother. I'm a little scared to read it. According to Jasper, anyone with eyes can see that I have a thing for Ellie. My mother has eyes in the back of her head, so if there is anything to see, she will be certain to see it.

We met Ellie today. I can see why
you are all so smitten.

She is a very lovely human girl.

I love you.

I love you too mom, tell dad I say HI!

Janeal just wants me to text her when we are coming back so that she can stock our food up. Ember wants to reschedule our date. I ignore them both.

Jasper walks into my room from his adjoining room. "All this blood is never going to come out of my jeans. Do ya think the front desk clerk got her color back yet?"

When we approached the front desk covered in blood, the poor clerk nearly fainted. We had to tell her the whole story about fighting a wolf. Luckily, the local news station was already covering the story, so we didn't have to make another trip to the local police station.

"That poor woman," I say, smiling and shaking my head. "I'm sure this little town has never seen so much action."

"They'll be telling the story of the wolf wrestlers for generations," he says flexing his biceps. "We're famous!"

Even two more bodies and a rogue alpha can't bring Jasper down.

"How's your not girlfriend?" he asks with a smile. I want to punch him but I'm too tired to deal with his shit.

"I don't have a girlfriend, Jasper," I say as I plop onto my bed and give him a mean stare.

"Oh really," he says, waving his phone at me, "Because your mom sure thinks you do."

"Well then, be sure to let my mom know that you introduced yourself to the 'lovely human girl' by dropping your towel at her," I say. I fluff my pillows and make a show of it so that Jasper will leave me alone and I can go to sleep.

"Your dear mom just wants me to tell her the truth," he says with a mock frown. "She's afraid that you're secretly dating the human, and she's scared she won't get giant meathead pups to bounce on her knee. She told me to push you toward Ember, she's a strong wolf girl."

"Great," I say, rolling away from him, "You date Ember. I'll stay single. Good night."

Jasper laughs as he walks back to his own bed, "You're grumpy when you're tired."

"Or maybe it's that I almost got eaten by a rogue alpha, then arrested by human cops," I snap.

"Nah," he says, "I don't think that's it. I think you miss your not-girlfriend."

He quickly protects his face as I chuck a pillow at his head. It hits his arms with a thud and falls to his chest.

My phone dings, and I swipe it from the nightstand before Jasper can grab it:

I'm glad to hear that you are both OK.

I'm sorry. Did I wake you?

No, I'm just doing some reading.
I'm guessing it didn't go as well
as you hoped?

Not even close. My day was shit,
so let's talk about yours instead.

You mean my day with a surprise
meeting of your parents.

I should have told you, I'm sorry.

It's OK, I can handle myself.

I have no doubts about that. Did they
give up any of my embarrassing secrets.

148

*Are you kidding, we busted out the
naked baby photos and everything.*

*Wow, you must have made quite the
Impression, Mom usually saves those
for after the 5th date.*

I immediately regret it. Why would I say that? What is wrong with
me? This is Jay's fault. He filled my head with this crap.

So, Mom and Dad didn't scare you off.

*Candy helped. Your dad seemed
really interested in my work.
We talked a lot.*

*He may be retired, but he is still a
leader at heart. Mom?*

She was nice.

*Is that code for she cornered you and
begged you to leave the community?*

*Haha. She doesn't like humans
much, huh?*

*She fears them. I'm really sorry if
she gave you a hard time.*

*She isn't the first to distrust
me when we first meet. I'm
sure that she'll come around.*

Thank you!

For what?

*For being you and giving her the
benefit of the doubt.*

Chapter Eighteen

We traveled back to the woods near the RV park. There were still way too many people around for us to work. The police and local hunters are combing the woods for the 'rabid' wolf.

If we shift and try to track Roberto in our wolf forms, we run the risk of getting shot by one of the trigger-happy locals. We'll never catch up to him in our human forms.

Another setback thanks to the local P.D. We'll just have to figure out another way to track him.

We've lost the element of surprise now, and I don't think he'll be dumb enough to use the pack's credit card again. The local police believe the body in the cabin is Roberto, so we don't have any leads there either.

Jasper and I need to come up with a plan.

We head to the local hospital where they are keeping the body from the cabin. Jasper charms a nurse into letting us see our "friend" to say goodbye.

Once we are alone, we use a stamp pad and some index cards we picked up at a drugstore to pull fingerprints from the dead man.

I'll send a picture to Ellie and see if she can get an ID from the FBI database. It's a long shot, but it is the only thing we've got right now. If we can figure out who this man is, maybe we can figure out why Roberto killed him. If he looked similar, maybe he plans to use this guy's identity in the next state.

We get the prints off to Ellie and she promises to send me whatever she can find.

In the meantime, Jasper and I head back to our hotel to work on the Iceland pack angle.

The Icelandic pack is relatively small and prefers to stay to itself. It is mostly thick-bloods, which means it is made up of almost all alpha-worthy wolves. They rarely marry outside their small pack and almost never welcome new members. They are a bit snobbish about their pure blood and don't want to mix it with the weaker blood of most of the other pack's members.

Maybe, the centuries of breeding among only a few bloodlines wasn't such a good idea. Perhaps, it is why we now have a deranged killer on the loose.

Just a thought.

Our discussion with the Iceland pack alpha goes just about as well as we thought it would.

"Olf," I say. "This guy had to come from your pack. Are you missing any members? Did you notice any pack males who seemed really angry with human women? Anything that you know could help us."

Olf flat-out denies that any of his pack would even leave Iceland. Let alone fraternize with humans.

"What about your more remote families?" Jasper tries. "Could they have hidden an unwell male from your pack? This guy is big and strong, Olf. He took on me and Bo and walked away without a scratch. Are you telling me that doesn't sound like an Iceland wolf? Everyone knows that you have the strongest wolves."

I give Jasper a thumbs up. Playing to Olf's pride is a great move. It's so easy for me to forget that he is an amazing leader and politician in his own right.

Olf pauses for a moment. "We do have the strongest wolves, best bloodlines in the realm."

Jasper and I are on the edges of our seats. Please, give us something to go on. Anything.

After a few moments, Olf tells us that he will call us back. He'll ask around the different tribes within his pack. Maybe one of them is missing a male.

Jasper and I thank him for any help he can give us. However, after we hang up with Olf, we still don't feel any better about our situation.

"What do you think our next move is?" I ask Jasper.

"I have no idea," he replies. "I guess we'll hang around here for at least another day. If we don't come up with anything, we'll have to head back and regroup from homebase."

I hate the idea of running away when we know we are so close to him. But Jasper has a point. We can't just aimlessly search the country for this man. It's unlikely that he'll hang around here knowing that we are on his tail.

Unfortunately, if Olf can't give us something or Ellie can't find anything on this dead man's prints, we'll just have to wait for our killer to strike again to give us a new trail to follow.

"I really hate this," I say to Jasper. "I feel like we should've had him. Goddamn local yocals."

"I know," Jasper replies somberly. "We had him right in our hands. But we did the right thing by protecting the humans. That's the whole point, right? We keep our secret. We protect our people by keeping them hidden in plain sight. We couldn't let him kill those people, and we couldn't shift in front of them. So, we were stuck doing the best we could with our human forms."

I know that Jasper's right. But it's so goddamn frustrating.

If we could have just taken off after him into the woods. We definitely could have taken him. Even as big as that guy is, he's no match for Jasper and me. Especially not in our wolf forms. We almost had him in our human forms, with an audience of humans keeping us from using any wolf power.

"Don't worry, bro," Jasper says, slapping me on the shoulder before plopping down on my bed next to me. "We'll get this asshole wolf, whatever it takes."

Again, I know that Jasper's right. I know that we'll get him. But I can't help but think, how many more bodies will have to fall before we catch him?

※

It's close to dinner time by the time Ellie calls me with her findings. She was able to identify the man that Roberto killed. He's a truck driver named Ray Stevens. It turns out he was staying close by at a local truck stop.

"So, this psycho probably has his hands on an 18-wheeler," I say to Ellie.

"No, Ray drove a smaller truck," Ellie replies. "It's still big, but it doesn't have a removable trailer. I think they're called box trucks. But, anyway, now that I have Ray's identity, I can flag his credit cards. They'll still work, but they'll let me know the moment they're used. This way he thinks he's still off our radar. Maybe he'll get lazy, and we can catch up to him."

Involving Ellie in the hunt for a bloodthirsty alpha wolf makes me strangely uncomfortable. He's dangerous. Much more dangerous than I had initially thought. Even though she is safely tucked away in my pack lands, I still feel a strange need to keep her protected.

That crazy wolf saw my face. If he recognized me as the Americas Alpha, he could try to strike back at me through my pack.

Another thought strikes me. Why was Roberto trying to change his identity again so fast? The cops only tied the fake Roberto to the girl in the woods because of their shared cause of death. Had he just moved on, they would have never even looked at him. They believe that the girl was killed by a wolf, not a murderer. He had no reason to burn that identity unless he thought that someone was looking into it.

"Ellie, I don't want you to talk to anybody but me or Jasper about this case, OK?" I say to her.

"OK," Ellie says a little hesitantly. "Do you think there is somebody on the inside giving him information?"

"I don't know yet," I say to her. "We think he's from the Iceland pack, which means he is as strong as any alpha throughout the world. Iceland is a very closed pack with some backward ass archaic ideas about selective breeding. There are always a few purest wolves in every community who believe that all the packs need to strengthen our community like the Iceland pack does. He could have allies that we aren't aware of."

"I don't understand what that means," Ellie says to me with a bit more edge to her voice. "Do you think that members of your pack are in danger from some kind of purest uprising?"

"I have no reason to believe that right now," I say to her as reassuringly as I can muster. "I just don't want to take any chances with you being a human and in a high-ranking position within my pack. Iceland wolves are notoriously anti-human, and I don't want to give anyone the opportunity to leak information about you being involved with this. I don't think anyone in my pack is involved in this, but I certainly don't want anyone accidentally leaking information to this guy."

For once in his life, Jasper holds his tongue, but I can feel his gaze boring into me.

After I hang up with Ellie, Jasper looks at me with the most serious look that I think I've ever seen him wear.

"That was smart," he says.

"I thought, for sure, you would bust my balls about it," I say to him.

"Oh, I will," Jasper replies. "Just not until we get this son of a bitch. It's smart not to take any chances with Ellie's life. We don't know anything about this guy except that he's killing human women. And now he knows that we're hunting him. And the only human woman that we have is Ellie."

I hadn't even considered that. If this guy is after human women because he believes that they did something wrong to him, then Ellie could be the crown jewel for him, especially considering that I'm the one hunting him.

The Iceland pack might be notorious for its dislike of all humans, but they never hurt them. Usually, they just ignore them. So, what changed for this guy? Why go after human women all over the world? Something must have happened; there has to be a trigger to make him act out like this.

Jasper and I decide that, without any other leads to follow, we'll head over to the truck stop. With any luck, our wolf still thinks that we're in jail or too stupid to figure him out. Maybe he's still there, sleeping it off in the truck, trying to recuperate. At the very least, I would take an eyewitness who saw which way he drove off.

When we get to the truck stop, we find that Ray's truck has already left. It's not surprising, but still disappointing. We do find someone who saw Roberto loading up on beef jerky and chips. Our witness thinks he heard him ask which way to Interstate 25. He only noticed the question because it was odd for a truck driver who was at this rest stop not to know how to get back to the interstate.

A quick look at our maps shows that Interstate 25 runs north and south. Our guy could be headed to Mexico or the Canadian wilderness, where we might never find him.

While we are walking around the truck stop, I notice that most of these trucks have transponders in the windows. It gives me an idea, if this guy's truck belongs to a company, it might have a GPS chip on it.

I call Ellie and ask her to text me all the details she can find about the trucking company that our victim, Ray, worked for.

I lay out my plan to her and Jasper.

"I'll call the truck company saying I'm from Homeland Security. Since Ray's truck was pretty close to the Mexican border, I'll say that we have reason to believe that he has Mexican thugs of some kind stowed away in his truck. I'll tell them that we need to access the GPS information for that truck without alerting the driver in any way. I'll tell them that these guys are serious, and they will kill their driver the moment they even suspect that he is deviating from his original plan. Then, I will have the truck company send Ellie a link to remotely access their GPS program, and from there, she can keep us posted as to where that truck is going."

Jasper nods in approval. "Be honest, Ellie, did you help him with this plan? I can't believe meathead came up with this all on his own."

It's a solid plan, and with Ellie's Homeland Security credentials, we should be able to execute it without an issue. No one knows what Homeland Security does; they just know that they don't want to be on their radar, so they comply in the hopes that we will quietly disappear when we have what we need.

Two hours later, and we're set up with the truck's GPS information. Roberto was never on Interstate 25. Instead, he got onto Interstate 40 and headed east.

Chapter Nineteen

Catching up with a large truck is harder than you think. We can't risk being delayed by getting pulled over, so we have to stay close to the speed limit. The box truck has a large gas tank, and our new rental SUV forces us to stop every few hours.

But we have his signal, and as long as he is moving, we know that he isn't hurting anyone.

Just inside Oklahoma, Ellie calls to let us know that Roberto has changed course and is now heading north on I-35.

"Do you guys think he has a plan?" Ellie asks. "Or is he just driving aimlessly?"

"We have no idea," I say. "We're hoping that Olf gets back to us today with this guy's real name. Maybe, if we can identify him, we can find out who he knows, or why he's doing this, and use that information to help catch him."

"Yeah," Jasper chimes in. "Because this chase game is bullshit. I'm not built to be cooped up in a car all day. I'm about to shift and stick my head out the window like a giant golden retriever."

Hearing Ellie laugh takes some of the heaviness out of my chest.

Obviously, I want to catch this guy to stop his madness, but it's more than that now. I also want to catch him because I'm eager to get back home to see Ellie. Leaving her alone in an unfamiliar community after I uprooted her entire understanding of the world around her was a shit move. It gives me a weird sort of empty feeling in my gut when I think about it, which is a lot.

Driving the interstate isn't that interesting, and I find my thoughts drifting to her more and more throughout the day. What is she doing now? Is Janeal keeping her company? Have any of the pack men noticed her yet?

When I left, her home was still weeks away from completion. Luna, please don't let it be finished before we return home. I need more time with her in the house. How stupid is that? I know nothing can come of it, but Ellie's presence gives me this strange sort of comfort. I've felt more alive over the last few weeks than I have in years.

Don't get me wrong, I have a great life, and I love it, but it just seems a little brighter these days.

Her scent makes the house feel warmer, somehow.

A phone call interrupts my wandering thoughts. Surprise makes my brows lift, it's Olf.

Jasper quickly answers the call on the SUVs dashboard. "Olf," he says. "How are you friend?"

Olf doesn't waste any time, "I do this for my pack. I have had time to think about your words, and, if this man is killing human women so recklessly, he puts us all at risk. This man you seek, his name is Ivor. He is my brother. I did not know he was doing these things. He tells me that he is going to travel to Norway to seek a wife."

"Olf," I say, "Do you have any idea why he is doing this? Or where he might go in the United States?"

Olf tells us that, since we talked, he heard from the local human village that Ivor had been having an affair with a human woman. Apparently, they were in love and decided to run away to be married. Olf's pack is strictly forbidden from *any* kind of relationship with a human, even business dealings.

When Ivor left the pack to marry her, he knew that he would never be able to return.

"Ivor has confessed his crimes to me," Olf says. "He tells me that the human rejected him when he offered her his blood to make her a wolf. He wanted to start a new pack. In his rage, he kills her. Now, in grief, he goes crazy."

Jasper and I are stunned.

"What do you mean he confessed to you?" Jasper asks. "You spoke to him?"

"Of course, I speak to him," Olf says. "I cannot give you my brother without knowing the truth."

My stomach sinks. "Olf, does Ivor know we are chasing him? Does he know who we are?"

Olf confirms that Ivor guessed that I was the alpha from the U.S. pack. He immediately recognized Jasper as the German pack leader and our head alpha. Olf confirmed for him that I was, indeed, the North American pack leader.

"Do you know where he is going?" I ask Olf.

"I do not," Olf says. "He doesn't tell me anything other than he is angry, and when he sees a human woman, if she smiles at him or talks with him, he gets very angry. Then he must kill her. He says he cannot stop. Any woman who tries to be with a wolf must be killed."

We thank Olf for his help and hang up.

I feel like I swallowed a large stone. My stomach is sick and heavy. Where is he going? Does this sudden turn North mean that he is headed to Oregon?

"Thank Luna, we didn't tell Olf anything about the truck driver or the GPS," Jasper says, breaking my thoughts.

He's not wrong. We still have an advantage. Ivor doesn't know that we are tracking him through the truck he is driving.

We call Ellie to update her on our new information, and she says that she was about to call us. Ivor has gotten onto I-70 and is headed west.

"Now that we know for sure that he's from the Iceland pack," I say. "And that he is the alpha's brother, we know just how serious this is. Ivor could be getting help from wolves all over the world. The Iceland pack is beloved by old-school wolves who believe in keeping the bloodlines strong and staying completely away from humans."

"But," Ellie says, "won't they feel betrayed by Ivor for trying to marry a human?"

Jasper answers, "I doubt he'll be telling them that part of the story. Or he'll find a way to twist it so that he is the unwitting victim of a wicked human woman. Purists don't come right out and condone violence against humans, but they don't exactly abolish it either. They don't think we should have to hide our existence. Their thoughts are that, if humans are scared of us, then let them be scared. And if they start a war, we fight back."

"Wow," Ellie says. "So, this has the potential to get even uglier. He could potentially cause a civil uprising among the purists and use them as a shield. With our attention turned to them, he can slip away and hide somewhere. It's a common tactic among rebel leaders."

"Beauty and brains," Jasper says while looking directly at me. "I'm telling you Ellie, Germany would be happy to have you. I'd make you a princess among my people."

I know he is just trying to get a rise out of me. I won't take the bait. We have larger concerns right now than me and Ellie.

"Ignore him," I say. "We'll call you later. Unless Ivor gets off the highway, then let us know right away."

After hanging up the phone, I turned to Jasper. "We should see if we can get that program loaded on one of our phones. We can't keep her chained to a desk watching the screen 24 hours a day."

He agrees. Jasper doesn't say it, but I think he is also worried that Ivor is headed for Ellie. Our human ambassador was big news for the pack. If Ivor has any friends within my pack, he could know that Ellie is there and alone.

"We have an advantage," Jasper says. "He'll have to stop at some point to sleep. There are two of us, so we can catch up to him while he sleeps and, maybe, if we're lucky, catch him off guard and take him down quickly and quietly."

"You better try to sleep for a while," I say to Jasper. "When you wake up, we'll trade off. This way we're both rested when we get to him."

※

As predicted, Ivor stops around 10 p.m.

While he is stopped, we pull over too. Ellie walks us through loading the GPS program onto my phone. Jasper takes over driving and I climb into the back seat to get some sleep.

In a few hours, we'll take Ivor down for good.

Jasper wakes me as we are pulling into the rest stop. We can see the truck pretty clearly from where we're parked. He parked it up right near the tree line. We'll use the small woods for cover when we approach the truck.

Jasper and I are deathly silent as we round the rest area through the trees. We both use our wolf senses to hear and see clearly in the dark. Coming up to the cab of the truck, something doesn't smell right.

I nod at Jasper, indicating that he sniffs.

He shakes his head at me, confirming that he doesn't smell Ivor either. This truck smells like a human, and not the cleanest one either.

Stalking up to the truck's driver-side door, I bang on the metal hard enough to leave dents. "Hey, Ivor, you in there, buddy?"

"Aye," a voice yells out, and the driver's door starts to open. "You must be my relief drivers."

Jasper and I look at each other, stunned.

"Your what?" Jasper says.

"My relief drivers," he says, looking back and forth between the two of us. "Ray said you'd meet me once I stopped. Paid me $300 to drive until I was too tired. Then he said you guys would show up in a couple of hours to take over. Said you'd give me some more cash to get home."

I grab the guy by the shirt, "Where?" I yell in his face.

Jasper grabs me by the shoulder and pulls me back from the innocent human.

"Take a walk," Jasper says to me, quietly but firmly. "I'll get all the information. Just go cool down, now."

Jasper might be the leader of our packs, but he isn't one to make demands of people, especially not of me. I do what he says and head toward the small woods.

It doesn't take too long before Jasper is walking up to me. "Apparently, our new human friend was standing around outside of a fast-food restaurant when 'Ray' ran up to him with a sob story about needing to get to his wife. He gave the guy a few hundred bucks to keep the truck moving toward California until we caught up to him. Told him we would be tracking him with GPS, so don't worry about the route. Or which rest area he stopped at. Just told him to drive until he couldn't drive anymore and that we would find him, pay him, and take over the truck."

"So, Ivor could be anywhere, and he has almost a full day's head start on us," I say, rubbing my hands down my face. "Fuck!"

Chapter Twenty

Jasper and I check into the closest hotel we can find. We are somewhere outside of Denver. We lost Ivor over 10 hours ago in Oklahoma City. He must have figured out that we were tracking him after he spoke to Olf.

We'll fly out of Denver tomorrow and go back to my pack.

"We're back to square fucking one," I say, throwing my bag on one of the double beds. "Olf is lucky I don't fly to Iceland tonight and rip his head off myself."

Jasper is quieter than normal. He's pissed off too. We really thought we had him, and that asshole played us.

"First thing in the morning," I say, "I'll have Ellie check Ray's cards. But if he knew we were tracking the truck, I doubt he'd use the cards. Maybe she can see if Ray, Roberto, or Ivor booked any flights, buses, or train tickets. I can't fucking believe he ducked us."

Jasper sits on the edge of his bed. "Let's just get some sleep. There's nothing else we can do tonight. He's a step ahead of us right now, but we'll find him. He told Olf that he can't help himself. So, he'll do it again. We just have to find an animal attack and we can start tracking him again."

I can't believe that we are just sitting around waiting for him to attack, and probably kill, another human woman. He outsmarted us and we fell for it. We underestimated him this time. I won't make that mistake again.

I'm still raging, so I stomp away to take a shower before bed. When I emerge, Jasper is there with a beer in each hand. Holding one out to me, he says, "Spill it?"

"What," I say, taking the beer.

"Whatever it is that has you this worked up," he says. "I'm upset that he played us, but you are well beyond your normal level of pissed."

I sit down on the bed close to Jasper. Our wolf instincts demand physical closeness with our family and loved ones, especially when we are emotional. We really are pack animals, and the thought that a member of my own pack might be giving Ivor information about our movements is tearing me up inside.

I lay out my theory to Jasper about Ivor getting tipped off about us coming to New Mexico, and about us following him in the truck.

"I can't imagine someone close to you doing that," Jasper says. "But it does explain Ivor's actions. Let's get some rest, we're heading back to your pack tomorrow morning, so we can work this angle from the inside and we'll keep an extra close eye on Ellie."

※

Ellie can't find a paper trail for Ivor.

Olf tells us that he tried calling his brother again, but the phone he had been using is disconnected now.

Ivor is covering his tracks. He knows that we are talking to Olf, that we know his name, and that we are on his trail. He won't be easy to find now.

The only thing that's keeping my mood up is that we'll be landing at the Ulfserkir airstrip in about an hour.

Three days of Jasper, cramped spaces, and fast food have me eager to get home. I can't wait for a home-cooked meal and my own bed. That last hotel probably gave me fleas.

I've been ignoring my messages from my mother and Ember for the last few days, but I had better start answering them, or no doubt, my mother will be on my doorstep demanding answers.

So I start with my mother:

I stopped at the store and saw Ember.
She says you're avoiding her. She's a really
nice girl, a good wolf. I like her a lot.

Don't worry. I smoothed it over with her.
I let her know that you are out hunting a rogue
wolf and haven't been able to call her.

That wasn't necessary, I will message
her today and let her know that I am
not interested.

Why?

I know it isn't because of Ellie. She
told Ember that you two simply
work together. I believe the phrase
she used was 'barely friends.'

It has nothing to do with Ellie.
I just don't want to date right now.
I am kind of busy with pack business.

This is already exhausting. I look up to see Jasper smiling at me. A big dopey smile that makes me want to punch him in the nose.

"You OK?" he asks. "Your thumbs were moving so fast I thought you'd break your phone screen."

"We're out here chasing a killer," I say, throwing my hands in the air. "And my mother is demanding I take Ember out on a date because she is a 'nice wolf.' Can you believe this shit? She went and talked to her at the store she works in."

Jasper looks at me expectantly. He shrugs his shoulders. "And? That sounds exactly like what I'd expect from your mother. Why is it bothering you so much now? Did she bring up Ellie?"

"Yes," I say defensively. "But that's got nothing to do with it. She knows the pack comes first. I'm busy right now. I just brought our first human ambassador to the pack lands, I'm chasing a killer alpha wolf, and she wants to know why I'm not texting Ember back."

"You have a point," Jasper says. "But all I really want to know is what she said about Ellie."

I read him the messages straight from my phone.

"Ouch," he says, making a grimacing face like he just watched me get punched. "Just barely friends, huh? No wonder you're so cranky."

"That has nothing to do with it," I say. "Ellie's right. We barely know each other. This is about my mother butting into my personal life. She is an alpha's wife. She knows how much I've been working lately. Besides, I wasn't interested in Ember even before I met Ellie, it has nothing to do with her."

"OK," Jasper says.

"Ember just isn't my type, OK," I say. "She's all about sun dresses and flower arrangements and brunch. It's just not what I'm into."

"OK," Jasper says again.

"I'm serious," I say. "If you like her so much, why don't you date her."

"Bro," Jasper says, holding his hands up in surrender. "All I said was OK."

"Keep it up," I say. "I'll tell my mom that you are too shy to ask her for help finding a wife. Then we'll see who's laughing."

Jasper's jaw drops open. "Yo, man, that's taking it too far. Don't you dare!"

We left our car at the airfield when we flew to New Mexico, so we don't need to wait for anyone to pick us up.

168

Jasper is still complaining about my threat. He hasn't had to fight off any wifely prospects from my mother in a while now. She's been too focused on me.

"You're driving," I tell him. "I have to text Ember and let her know that I'm not interested in dating right now."

"Fine," Jasper says, "but keep my name out of it."

As we pull away from the airfield, I stare at my phone and decide to read through Ember's texts.

> *Hey, this is Ember didn't know if you lost my number.*

> *Just thinking of you and wanted to say hi.* 😊

> *I met Ellie today, let me know if you want me to show her around.*

> *I heard you had to leave town, be safe.*

I feel awful, but it's better to let her down now than to lead her on. I wasn't lying when I told Jasper she isn't my type. Ember is the kind of girl who doesn't leave the house without a full face of make-up and her hair is always perfect.

I have no doubt that she's a great girl. But I just have no interest in her, I prefer a more natural look and a more carefree style.

It takes me almost the whole ride to find the right words.

> *Ember, I'm sorry I haven't gotten back to you. Pack business has kept me very busy. I'm glad you had a chance to meet Ellie. It's really up to her if you two get together. I don't have any say in what she does outside of work. I know I told you we would get together soon, but unfortunately Pack business has me way too busy right now. I won't be going out on any dates anytime soon.*

It's not my best work. But it's the best I can do right now. I really need to man up and go speak to her in person, but that will have to wait. To be honest, my tank is kind of empty. Ivor has got me off my game. I can't think straight with him out there Luna knows where, plotting Luna knows what.

I still can't believe how bad he played us. I need to focus all of my energy on finding him right now.

If we are really lucky, maybe he slipped up somewhere, and Ellie's got some leads for us.

It doesn't take long before we're pulling up to my house. We open the door, and I can already smell her. It takes a little bit of the weight off my shoulders.

Jasper gives me a knowing smile. Of course, he can smell her, too. I don't even care; there's nothing wrong with being happy about your home smelling so good. The truth is, Ellie's sweet citrus scent is better than any air fresheners or candles I've ever smelled.

He can't blame me for smiling at a sweet smell. Everyone likes their house to smell nice.

I can hear Ellie's footsteps upstairs, she heard us come in, so she must not have had those stupid noise-canceling earbuds in her ears. Coming down the stairs, she greets us with a huge smile.

"I'm so glad you guys are back safe," she says jogging down the stairs.

Jasper smiles widely at her. "Oh, come on," he says to her, grabbing her into a surprise hug and winking at me. "It takes more than one crazy wolf to take us out."

Ellie pulls out of Jasper's embrace and shakes her head. "I've been a nervous wreck since you two left. I hope this doesn't happen a lot. I don't think my nerves can take it."

To my surprise, Ellie hugs me in greeting as well and plants a soft kiss on my cheek.

Shaking my head, I say, "Don't worry. This is completely out of the ordinary. I usually leave Jasper at home."

Jasper punches me in the arm. "Oh, OK, so now you've got jokes Mr. Grumpy Ass."

"Seriously though," I say to her. "Thank Luna this doesn't happen often. This guy put up one hell of a fight. We totally underestimated him, physically and mentally. Not only did he fight off me and Jasper together, then he made us look like assholes chasing the wrong driver for 10 hours."

"First of all, it wasn't a fair fight," Jasper says in his normal jovial tone. "Ivor was in wolf form, and he used humans to distract us. Ivor doesn't know it yet, but he really messed up. He really pissed off Bo. Like, he's really pissed off. And that was not a great idea."

Ellie makes a mock scared face at Jasper and me. I can't help but smile at her.

"Well, I've been keeping an eye on all of Ray's credit cards," she says. "So far Ivor hasn't used anything. I'm still watching the pack's prepaid credit card, and I've requested a travel flag be put on every alias that we know about."

"I have to get to my laptop," I say. "I want to make sure I set up plenty of alerts for any animal attacks reported throughout the country."

The truth is, we have no idea where Ivor is. He sent us off course for over 10 hours, during which time he could've gone in any direction. We are now almost 36 hours behind him, and we have no idea which direction to go.

You can get pretty goddamn far in 36 hours.

"Well," Jasper says, "I think I'm gonna go up and take a shower. Get that nasty hotel off me. If I find you in the bathroom this time, Ellie, I'll know it wasn't an accident. And, like I said, only the first one is free."

Jasper winks at me and then jogs up the stairs two at a time.

Ellie covers her face with her hands, shaking her head. She's clearly still embarrassed about her first meeting with Jasper.

Turning her attention to me, Ellie says "OK what can I do to help?"

"Alright," I say to Ellie. "Let's start with the basics. Olf said that Ivor ran off with a human. He went nuts when she refused to take his blood and turn into a wolf."

"Wait," Ellie says, holding up her hands in a stop motion. "You can do that; you can give someone your blood and turn them into a wolf? Like, do they drink it?"

"Yes, we can make wolves," I say. "But no, you don't drink the blood. It's more like a transfusion. Technically, Ivor would have been making a sister, but the Iceland pack isn't too picky about that sort of thing."

Ellie scrunches her nose. "He would have been making his wife into his biological sister, ew. Do your people make humans into wolves a lot?"

"No," I say, shaking my head. "It's technically against our treaty with the humans, but very occasionally it has been done. It's generally frowned upon. In darker times, when an alpha didn't have a male heir, or needed a female heir for political marriages, they would steal or buy a human child and turn them into an heir. It was normal back then, but we have abolished that practice and outlawed it in every pack. But, between two consenting adults, it's a little harder to outlaw. But it's a dangerous practice, and not every human can handle shifting."

"Interesting," Ellie says. "OK, back to Ivor. So, his girlfriend rejects him, and then what?"

"That's just it," I say. "Olf says he killed her, but do we really trust him at this point? We don't know for sure what happened to her or anything between the rejection and when Jasper figured out that he had a killer on his hands. Maybe she's still alive, or maybe Olf was telling the truth and he killed her first. I'd like to know for sure either way. If she is alive, maybe she can tell us something. Why did Ivor go to Germany, why come here, where could he be going next?

Maybe he told her something? I know it's a long shot, but we've got nothing to go on. I can't just sit around and wait for more victims."

"OK," Ellie says. "I'll see what I can find out about her. I'll start by talking to the police closest to Olf's pack. Ivor would have had to meet this woman during his normal life, and from what I gather, he didn't go out of his way to meet humans. Maybe the police can tell me who the woman is and if she ever came back from her trip."

Checking the time, I tell her, "That'll have to wait until tomorrow. Iceland is 7 hours ahead of us. It's the middle of the night there."

Chapter Twenty-One

I'm feeling much better after a full night of sleep in my own bed.

I take my time showering and shaving before going downstairs. I need to reset so that I can start the search for Ivor again with a clear head.

Ellie and Jasper are at the dining table. I can hear her laughing all the way upstairs. Jasper isn't that funny. I wonder if she is attracted to him. Women laugh at bad jokes when they're attracted to a man, right?

I make my way to the coffee pot; I can hear their conversation now. Jasper is telling her about the fight with Ivor and how the local cops, and the poor hotel clerk, both got the scare of their lives seeing the two of us covered in blood.

"I've never been so happy to have human witnesses," Jasper says. "That cop was scared shitless when he saw me and big boy over there, covered in blood and pumped full of adrenaline. If those campers hadn't jumped to our defense, that guy would still be reloading and shooting at us. He couldn't have been more than 150 pounds soaking wet. There he is, staring at 450 pounds of pure rage. I can't even blame him."

Ellie is still giggling. She shakes her head and says, "I bet you guys were a sight to behold. Those people must have thought you were nuts. I bet you become folk legends down there."

Sliding into a chair, I say, "I think the night clerk at that hotel probably quit her job."

"That poor woman," Ellie says. Turning in her seat to face me, she says, "Now that you are here, let me fill you guys in on what I learned about Ivor's girlfriend."

"You spoke to the Iceland cops already?" I ask, a little shocked.

Ellie continues, "I called them at 8 a.m. their time. I wanted to find out as much as I could as soon as I could."

"Ellie," I say. "That's 1 a.m. our time."

She smiles sweetly, "I know. I was there."

Jasper has to turn away not to laugh. Facing me, he hides his smile behind his coffee cup.

"Anyway," Ellie continues, "the local police said that Ivor's girlfriend did return. They gave me her contact information. So, I called and spoke to her brother, and he convinced her to talk to me. According to Anna, Ivor was always talking about building a new pack, becoming larger and stronger than the other packs. Before they got to Norway, Anna didn't know that Ivor had wanted to make her a wolf. He told her that she could never join the pack as a human and that they needed to produce strong-blooded wolf boys. She says that he laid out a plan that included recruiting strong wolves from the other packs to come with him. They would return to the old ways, and no one would ever know that she had been a human. She says that after she told him that she didn't want to become a wolf, he started mumbling crazy things about a true wolf king and being the 'one,' but she doesn't know what he meant by any of it."

I take a moment to think it through. Anna didn't just reject Ivor, and reject becoming a wolf, she broke his dream of ruling a pack of thick-blooded wolves. He wanted to return to the old ways, but what does he mean by that? He can't shun humans with a human wife, but he also wanted to hide her lineage from his new pack. Was he planning to create a pack with human children? Nothing is adding up here.

I let out a long sigh. "I guess he went to Germany and then came here because that was part of his original plan. It worries me that he was so unhinged *before* losing his mind. Maybe he is still looking to make a human woman into his perfect wolf wife?"

Jasper raises an eyebrow. "I guess he could see a woman he likes, start talking to her, even date her, then if she does something that offends him or makes him believe that she will reject his wolf offering, he kills her. At least, that is probably how it started. Now, I think he is just killing any woman he finds attractive and not even waiting for her to upset him in any way. It's like he is unraveling."

"It's been almost 4 days since we caught him at that RV park,' I say. "Where the hell is he?"

Ellie reaches across the table and puts a hand on my forearm. "I know you'll find him, and I know you'll stop him," she says with a look of concern in her eyes.

Her hand is warm and soothing on my arm. It almost feels like she is lifting the weight right off of my shoulders. Looking down at her delicate fingers, I can't help but place my hand on top of hers and smile.

"Thanks," I say. "I just don't know how many more women Ivor will hurt, and I really can't stand that he outsmarted us."

I can sense Jasper's eyes on us. I quickly remove my hand from Ellie's. She seems to realize what is going on at the same time and quickly pulls her hand back as well.

"Anyway," I say quickly, "what's Janeal got in the fridge for breakfast?"

※

"It's been a week," I say to Jasper. "There has to be some sign of him somewhere."

We've been going through online news articles for hours every day. Once in the morning and again in the evening. We're looking for any suspicious animal-related deaths, anything that could have possibly been an animal attack, or any mutilation that might be a wolf attack.

Jasper rubs his eyes. "I've got a rabid dog in Central Park in New York, and a mountain lion in Happy Camp, California. What do you got?"

"I've got an unusually large Mexican wolf outside of Bamopa, but no attacks," I say. "Tell me more about New York."

Jasper summarizes the reports from New York. Looks like a medium-sized dog is chasing rollerbladers and bike riders. Nothing there for us, Ivor would never be described as a medium-sized dog, and he sure as hell isn't chasing bikes.

"OK," I say. "What about Happy Camp? Are we sure it's a mountain lion?"

According to Jasper, the details in the mountain lion case are thin. Rangers and police released their statement but didn't give details about why they believed it was a mountain lion.

A couple of phone calls later, and we have some doubts about the mountain lion story. We couldn't get a whole lot of information out of the rangers over the phone, but we got enough to know that they didn't think that the prints matched a cougar and that there was a second set of human footprints that were too large to be the female victim's feet.

"Up for a road trip," I say to Jasper. "We can try to get a look at the scene, maybe even catch a scent. My phone says it's about 7 hours in the car."

"Beats sitting around here all day watching you pretend that you're not staring at Ellie," Jasper says.

"I don't stare," I say defensively. Falling into the Jasper trap once again.

"OK," Jasper says. "And I guess you don't keep tabs on her every movement either."

"No," I say. "I don't keep tabs on her. I just pay attention, that's all. Ellie always tells *both* of us where she is going. Does that mean that you're keeping tabs on her, too?"

"Bro," Jasper says, shaking his head at me. "I don't get it. Why can't you just admit that you like her? You're an adult, you're the alpha of the pack, and she clearly likes you. What are you afraid of?"

Standing from my desk, I let out a frustrated sigh. "Hasn't this entire thing with Ivor shown you why it's a bad idea for humans and wolves to be together?"

Jasper throws his hands over his head. "Are you serious, you are going to use Ivor going insane and killing humans as an excuse for not growing some balls and making a move on Ellie. I want you to take her to dinner, bang her, whatever. I'm not telling you to tie her up and make her a wolf."

I give Jasper a sharp look. "Don't talk like that about Ellie. She's not some rando chick to play around with. Show some fucking respect."

"You see what I mean," he says, leaning toward me and smiling. "That, right there, that is you telling everyone that you really like her. You care about her, man. So why not? You deserve to be happy."

I grab my charge cord and start packing up my laptop to take with us on the trip. "Why are you so obsessed with this? Just leave it alone. I have obligations to the pack. I can't throw the rules aside because I'm the alpha. I lead by example and follow my own pack laws."

"You're an idiot," Jasper says. "Everyone knows that you want Ellie, except maybe Ellie. The pack is already talking about it. Why do think your mom is so up your ass about dating someone, anyone? She wants to stop the rumors that you two are already together. Your mom knows that you'll never marry Ember. Even Chester knew that. He only set you up with her because his girlfriend made him do it."

"I can't break pack laws," I say. "I won't do it. I have to hold myself to the same standard that I hold every other wolf to. And how do you know that about Chester? Are you talking to people about me and Ellie behind my back?"

"Oh, shut up," Jasper says, "What are you, a 15-year-old girl? I'm not talking about you behind your back, Nancy. Besides, I think that this whole business with Ivor is a great reason to revisit pack laws. Maybe it's time we take a second look at our policies regarding human/wolf relationships. Perhaps we should keep the rules about telling humans who don't know about us the same, but amend the rules for those who already know."

I am trying to walk away and end this conversation, but Jasper is following me around the house while I pack for our road trip.

"Jay," I say, turning to face him. "Now isn't the time. Go pack yourself a bag and get the hell away from me."

"Fine," he says, "but we are going to pick this conversation up in the car. You can't dodge me forever. Whether you like it or not, I'm the big cheese, and I can raise these concerns in my official capacity as high alpha. As my second, you have to listen."

I smile, "I might not be able to get away from you inside the car, but I *can* leave you on the side of the road in bumfuck northern California."

Chapter Twenty-Two

As promised, Jasper spends most of the 7-hour drive talking about how he would amend the policies surrounding interspecies relationships in our treaty and pack laws.

He comes off as a playboy, but Jasper is actually a damn good alpha. He took over as alpha after his parents died in a car accident 6 years ago. At least when I took over for my own father 5 years ago, I still had him here to help me. Jasper had to jump into the role feet first, on his own.

Of course, my father also helped him as much as he could, but Jasper had to prove himself to his people on his own.

As much as I hate to admit it, he made some valid points on the drive. It was the complete outlawing of wolf/human relationships that started the ball rolling for Ivor. To be with the woman he loved, he had to leave his pack for good.

Without his pack to fall back on for support, he broke under the weight of his lover's rejection. He couldn't move forward with her unless she became a wolf, and when she was too scared to take that chance, he snapped.

Jasper theorizes that if Ivor had been able to stay with the pack, declare his love for Anna, and then work with the pack to bring her into wolf life, maybe none of this would have happened. Maybe Anna would have never become a wolf, maybe she would have, but Ivor would have had his family around him and would not have become an outcast.

Even though Jasper's constant talking did make the drive go by faster, I'm not convinced that Ivor's rampage is motivated by a broken heart, or that having his pack to fall back on would have made a difference.

By the time we are pulling into the parking lot, I'm thankful we have arrived at the ranger station and Jasper will be forced to stop talking.

We manage to convince the rangers that we're FBI agents who believe that there is a killer covering up his tracks by making his kills look like animal attacks. They agreed to talk to us "off the record" because, according to our cover story, our bosses don't buy our theory and don't want us involved.

Their willingness to help shows me that there's a lot more to this scene than we've learned from the official reports.

The rangers take us to the area where the woman was found. It's remote and not easy to get to. While we hike, the rangers fill us in on what they know about the woman.

Apparently, she was an avid hiker who went to the trails almost every day. In the days before her disappearance, she told friends that she could sense something watching her when she hiked.

When we get to where she was found, there is still a lot of blood along the rock.

"Do we know how long she was here before she was found?" I ask.

"We think she was here for 2 days," the ranger says. "Based on what we can tell, it was 3 days ago the last time she was seen."

"Why don't you guys walk us through what you found?" Jasper says. "And don't leave out anything weird. We know this scene didn't add up for you, so tell us everything."

The two rangers look at each other, and then the older one starts to tell us about the scene. The woman was badly mauled. But the prints looked like giant wolf prints, and then there were human footprints that fell right in line with the wolf prints.

"I could see some of the bite marks," the younger ranger says. "They were too big to be wolves, but not the right shape for a cougar."

Bite marks? Ivor has never bitten a victim before. Is he unraveling under the pressure?

The younger ranger seems convinced that someone tried to make it look like an animal attack, but that they didn't make their bite marks correctly and got sloppy with their footprints.

"Plus," the older ranger says, "we haven't found her car yet."

Jasper and I are convinced that it's Ivor. We get the details from the rangers about the woman's identity and what kind of car she drives.

I text Ellie with an update.

> *It's Ivor. He's got a car and 3*
> *days head start. We are only a*
> *half day from you and he's had 3.*
> *I need you to be extra careful.*
> *Don't go anywhere alone*

> *Do you really think he would come here?*

> *I don't know but I don't have a*
> *good feeling.*

> *When will you be back?*

> *We are leaving here now. We are*
> *coming straight back to the house.*

> *OK, I'll see you soon. Be safe*

> *Lock the doors and windows and*
> *keep those damn earbuds in the*
> *case!*

> *Yes dad* 😵

> *This is serious. He's hunting*
> *human women.*

> *He's not my first terrorist.*

ELLIE – lock the doors and
windows!!!

> *I'm doing it now. Don't worry,*
> *just drive safe.*

Jasper and I climb into the car, he drives while I make some phone calls. I need to update the Pack Squad and my council about the threat to our land.

I start with the Pack Squad commander. He hasn't heard anything about unusual scents in the borders, but he'll put the word out to all squad members to report anything and everything that might be out of place.

Next, I conference Chester, Candy, and Roman. I update them on Ivor and my growing worry that he is coming for me and Jasper.

"I think he wants to finish what we started at the RV park," I tell them. "We surprised him at home, and now he wants to surprise me at mine."

We are all worried about the outlying community members. He'll have to pass by hundreds of women and children to get to my house. And then there's Ellie. She's in my house, she's alone, and she's human.

Roman and Chester decide to go to the house and watch over things. When he shifts, Roman is the size of a grizzly bear and easily just as strong. Chester is smaller, but there isn't a faster wolf out there.

I feel much better knowing that they will be there with Ellie, but I still have to fight the urge to yell at Jasper to drive faster.

He senses my unease, not that it's hard to pick up on, and tries to reassure me. "It's us he wants," Jasper says. "Even if he scents Ellie, I don't think he'll move on her with Roman and Chester there. Even Ivor isn't stupid enough to poke the old bear."

On some level, I know that Jasper is right. Roman and Chester are formidable together. Speed and strength that are unmatched in any other duo, save Jasper and myself.

It isn't long before my phone is ringing. It's the Pack Squad commander. Maybe they caught Ivor. I answer the phone on speaker.

"Sir," the commander says. "I just heard back from one of our scout teams. They report scenting a strange alpha on the southwest border two days ago. They didn't make a report because they assumed it was Mr. Adolpha. I have put the entire Squad on high alert and called in every member to assist in tracking."

"Fuck," I yell. "Two days ago, and we are just hearing about it now. They better hope to Luna that there isn't a single casualty, or I swear they will answer directly to me. Get out to my house and assist Roman and Chester in protecting our human ambassador."

I hang up before he can answer. My hands are shaking with rage.

Jasper says, "You better call Roman and Chester with the update. Better they know that Ivor is likely already onsite."

Before I can compose myself enough to work my phone, it rings again. "It's Roman," I tell Jasper.

I answer the phone before the first ring stops, "Did you get to Ellie?"

Roman doesn't usually hesitate, and he's not one to sugarcoat, so when he says, "Bo, try not to worry, it's probably nothing," I immediately feel nauseous.

"What the fuck is going on," I say.

"Ellie isn't here, Bo." He says.

"What the fuck do you mean she isn't there? Where is she?" I'm yelling now.

Jasper grabs the phone from me. "Roman, it's Jasper. Tell us everything you see. If Ellie left the house on her own, she would have left a note on the kitchen island. Do you see anything there?"

Roman tells us that her laptop is open on the dining table, and next to it, there is a half-eaten sandwich and a cold glass of water. She couldn't have left that long ago.

"Ellie wouldn't leave her laptop open, and she definitely wouldn't leave food on the table," Jasper says. "Check every single room, she has noise-canceling earphones and when she uses them, she can't hear shit."

While Jasper is holding my phone, a text comes in from Ellie. I can see it from my seat.

> *Was it really necessary to send the*
> *inspector to bring me to my new*
> *house.*

"Roman," I yell. "Get to Ellie's house now. She just texted me that the inspector came by. There is no fucking inspector, it's got to be Ivor. Fucking find them, Roman."

Jasper tells Roman to call us back as soon as he finds anything.

I grab my phone and call the Pack Squad commander. I fill him in and order the Squad to fan out from my house and Ellie's.

I call Ellie. Voicemail. I text her.

> *Please call me!*

"I just fucking told her not to go anywhere alone, lock the doors and windows," I say, fear and frustration making me yell.

Jasper shakes his head, "She didn't go anywhere alone, she went with someone who she thought you sent to get her."

I don't know how long passes before Roman calls us back. It could have been a minute, but it felt like an hour. I have no idea.

"Bo," The old man says between huffing breaths. "We've got Ellie. She's fine."

Roman must have me on speaker because I hear Ellie speaking next.

"I'm sorry, I thought you sent him," Ellie is yelling now, too. "He said you sent him to check on me and take me to the house to hide."

I can hear the panic in her voice. I'll rip Ivor's head off his shoulders the next time I lay eyes on him. I don't care who is around to witness it.

"Don't let her out of your sight," I yell. "You don't let her get more than an arm's length from you! I'll be there in a few hours. The Squad should be there any second, you tell them to find that motherfucker."

Roman might be older, but he is a tactical fighter. At his suggestion, they bring Ellie back to the city office. My house is surrounded by wooded land. Ivor can sneak up on them from any direction. There is no chance he can sneak up on them in the office building; it is the safest option.

Jasper and I agree and say our goodbyes to Chester and Roman. Ellie is still apologizing when we end the call. I can hear the strain in her voice and it unlocks a rage in me that has me fighting not to shift in the front seat of the SUV.

※

We are almost to the pack border when Jasper finally speaks again. He says it, the question that has been hanging in the air for the last hour and a half.

"Why didn't he kill her?"

I take four deep breaths before I even try to talk.

"I don't know," I say. "I've been thinking about it the whole ride. Is it to taunt me? Was he interrupted? Was she just too fucking nice to him? What, what stopped him?"

"You couldn't have known that he would go there," Jasper says.

As my oldest friend, he knows that I'll blame myself for not seeing that Ellie was his next move, and I do. I knew he would go after her,

187

and I had a sick feeling in my stomach. I even told her to be careful. But I left anyway. I left her there unprotected.

"But I did know," I say. "And I still…I fucking left her there alone. What did I do to protect her? I texted her to lock the doors. What the fuck did that do? You want me to admit feelings for her and be a happy fucking couple. Dating me would paint a giant target on her back. I can't even protect her as a normal human guest on my land, how would I protect her as my girlfriend?"

Jasper, wisely, doesn't say anything about that. Instead, he turns his attention to Ivor.

"What's his move now? He gave away his advantage. We know he's close."

I lean back in my seat for the first time since speaking to Roman. "I don't know. But I'm going to fucking kill him for this."

Chapter Twenty-Three

When we pull up to the city office. There are a couple of PS members out front and more on the roof. Ivor probably won't be back today, but they aren't taking any chances. If Jasper is right, and the whole pack thinks I'm dating Ellie, then the PS are probably afraid that I'll come in here ready to kill them all for not protecting her in my absence.

The truth is, it wasn't their fault. I should have personally briefed them on Ivor and had Jasper with me so they would all have his scent.

It's my fault. I was too cocky. I didn't truly believe that Ivor would walk onto my land, let alone right up to my front door. I left Ellie alone thinking that Ivor wouldn't dare come to my house.

I swore that I wouldn't underestimate him again, but I did. That's twice now he's made me the asshole.

I nod at my men as I enter the building. Jasper is on my heels but has remained quiet. He knows that I'm in no mood for jokes right now.

We get out of the elevator on the fourth floor, and I see Roman and Chester talking to the PS Commander.

"Tell me everything we know," I say as I walk up to the men.

"Bo," Roman says, turning toward me and pulling me into a bear hug. "You're here. Good. Ellie is in your office if you would like to see her first."

"No," I say. "I need to know everything we know so far. I'm done with Ivor. He walked up to my front door. I'm going to find him and I'm going to kill him."

Roman nods and fills me in on the details.

"He came to the house and told Ellie that you had sent him to move her to the new house. She went with him on foot. She said that he was asking a lot of questions about why you would keep a human woman, and why she would agree to come here. She got suspicious and asked him what his real name was. He told her. She didn't panic, and he asked her if she was scared of him. She said no, that Anna had told her that he was a good man." Roman pauses. "She took a risk bringing up Ivor's human girlfriend."

I nod my head. "She's good under pressure, and her political experience has taught her how to judge people."

Roman continues. "She said they walked all the way to the house, and Ivor asked her questions about Anna. Ellie told him that she had spoken to Anna on the phone and that Anna misses him very much. She stalled him long enough that we were right behind them. He heard us coming and told her he would have to finish their conversation later."

I take a moment to process everything that Roman said. "Any luck picking up his trail?"

The Commander shakes his head. "No, sir. It seems that he spread his unwashed clothes all over the woods before approaching Ellie. His scent leads everywhere and nowhere."

"Tell your men to be on extra high alert," I say. "Three men to a patrol, no one goes anywhere alone. This guy is big, strong, and really smart. Anything even remotely unusual is to be reported immediately. I'm going to check on Ellie, and then Jasper and I will head to my house for some essentials. Ellie stays here until Ivor is caught. Patrols stay outside and on the roof."

I storm off to see Ellie in my office. I want to hear her story, look her in the eyes, and make sure she is OK. She's been our ambassador for a month, and she's already been kidnapped and almost killed.

"Ellie," I say softly as I open the office door. "Can I come in?"

"It's your office," she says in an unusually casual tone. "Of course, you can come in. Don't be silly."

I slip inside the office and quickly close the door behind me. Closing the gap between us, I instinctively grip Ellie up into a hug. "I'm so sorry, Ellie. I should have never left you alone. I promise I'll never put you in harm's way again, and I'll make Ivor pay for coming after you."

My words flow out of me in a rush. Seeing her in person and seeing that she really is okay feels like a physical weight has been lifted off my chest. It's like I am taking my first full breath in hours.

"It mote you alt," Ellie tries to speak, but her face is smooched into my shoulder.

I ease up my grip on her and let her take a step back.

"Sorry," I say. "I guess I was so relieved that Ivor didn't hurt you that I nearly squashed you to death myself."

"I said," Ellie says with a smile. "It's not your fault. You didn't make Ivor come after me. None of us saw this coming."

I run my hand through my hair and shake my head. "But I did see it coming. I knew he would come for you, I felt it, and I left anyway. If something would have happened to you, it would have been my fault."

"Don't be ridiculous," Ellie says with her hands on her hips. "Ivor is a maniac. You are not responsible for anything that he does. If Ivor could be controlled, then his brother would have controlled him. He is a grown man, making terrible choices. You are not responsible for that."

"Listen," I say, still not letting go of her upper arms. "I'm just so happy you are safe now. You're staying in this building until Ivor is caught. The PS couldn't track him. He left his clothes scattered around the woods so that his scent would be everywhere. He's smart."

"I know," she says, moving away and sitting on the edge of my desk. It's a very enticing sight, and the thoughts that run through my head are definitely not appropriate. I have to turn around and busy myself getting a drink from the wet bar.

"I've been thinking," Ellie continues. "How did Ivor know where to find me?"

"It's big news that a human ambassador was assigned to my pack," I say. "He could have heard it anywhere."

"Yeah," she says. "I get that. But he knew that I was staying at your house. He also knew that I was having a house built on your property. It's one thing for him to know there is a human here, but it is another to know exactly where I am and how to get me out of the house. This isn't a small town, and your house isn't flashy. There is nothing to suggest that anyone special owns that house."

"Right," I say. "How did he know which house was mine? He only had a couple of days between Happy Camp and showing up at my doorstep. It's a 7-hour drive. So, that gives him two days, tops, to find my house and figure out about your house, all without being detected by anyone. Then he just so happens to approach you while you are alone."

"Doesn't sit right, does it?" Ellie says with a smirk.

"Someone in my pack is definitely talking to him," I say in a tone that doesn't even come close to my actual anger level. To think that someone in my own pack put Ellie in danger, it makes me want to tear the city apart.

"The real problem," Ellie says, "will be trying to figure out who. Like you said, it's big news that I'm here. A lot of people in town know where I am. And they all know where you live."

I think about that for a moment. "That's true, but how many know that both Jasper and I were gone? We went to Happy Camp on a whim. Only a handful of people knew about it."

Ellie grabs a notepad. "OK, let's map it out. Who knew you were gone and who did they tell, or at least possibly tell?"

Janeal	Roman	Chester	Candy	Jasper
?	Francine?	Girlfriend?	Mom?	Mom?
?	Friends?	Ember?	Ember?	Ember?

"We need to talk to everyone and find out if they told anyone else," Ellie says.

I can't help but notice that she wrote Ember down three times. Pointing to the names, I ask, "Do you maybe think it was Ember?"

"I'm just mapping out people I know who have a connection," Ellie says. "Your mom brought up that they are friendly and often talk about you, so if Jasper or Candy told your mom, she might have told Ember. And of course, if Chester told his girlfriend, she might also have told Ember. It doesn't make Ember more of a suspect, just more likely that someone told her. I mean, your mom is on the list twice, but that doesn't mean that I think she is the mole."

I look around in mock conspiracy and lower my voice, "Well, Ember is my number one suspect. She is the only person I can think of who would want you gone."

"Me," Ellie says in a high-pitched voice. "Why? I never did anything to her."

"There is a good chance that she thinks that you are the reason that I won't date her," I say with a shrug.

"That's absurd," she says. "I don't have any say in who you date."

"Well," I say. "Apparently, there are a lot of people around here who think you do. The rumor is that we're dating."

"Why would anyone think that?" Ellie says, her eyebrows shooting to her hairline.

"Well," I say, shrugging, "you're a beautiful, intelligent woman, and you're living in my house. People assume that something must be going on. But I refused to date Ember before I even knew you."

"OK," she says. "But that is a far cry from helping a killer track me down. I've spoken to Ember myself; I told her that there isn't anything between us."

"Oh, yes," I say bitterly. "We're barely even friends, right?"

Ellie looks shocked by my statement, but it is only a momentary lapse in her normal, casual expression.

"Yes, I did say that. I mean," Ellie stammers. "When I spoke to her, I had only just gotten here. I didn't mean to imply that we didn't like each other; I just meant that we had just met and barely knew each other. I certainly didn't mean to offend you."

"So," I say. "Are you saying that you do like me now? That we are friends now?"

Ellie puts her hand on her forehead. "Are we really going to talk about this right now? I mean, seriously, what do you think this is, some cheesy romance novel? There is a crazy werewolf psycho-killer hunting me, who is bigger and stronger than everyone else, but let's take time to discuss whether or not I have a crush on you."

"Whoa," I say, putting up my hands to stop her in her tracks. "He isn't bigger or stronger than me."

I see a slight rush of red slide into Ellie's face. I have definitely managed to annoy her. I like it. She looks cute when she's angry.

"Really, that's all you heard?" She says.

"No," I say. "I also caught the crush on me part. But I'm just saying, just so you know, he isn't. But you're right. Our priority is Ivor and keeping you safe. I think I've been spending way too much time with Jasper. We'll all meet when I get back to start planning our next move."

Ellie frowns, "Where are you going? You just got here."

"I know," I say. "But I have to go to the house and get some things: clothes and toiletries for you and Jasper, your laptop, your yoga mat, some snacks—you know, the essentials."

She smiles at me and shakes her head, and I can tell, she totally likes me.

※

"Roman," I say when I leave my office. The old man makes it to me in just a few paces. He might be gray around the temples, but he is all warrior. He was literally built for this.

"We need to talk privately before I leave," I say, leaning in to whisper to him.

We duck into Roman's office and close the door.

I explain our theory that someone is feeding Ivor information from within our pack.

"From now on," I say. "We keep everything close to the vest. No one gets information about our whereabouts, not even Francine. We don't know where the leak is, so we have to shut it all down. Can you fill Chester in, too?"

Chapter Twenty-Four

Jasper and I make quick work of packing up all the supplies we need from my house. The office has four executive suites, each with its own shower. We will be able to stay there for a few days before it gets too uncomfortable.

"I just don't get it," Jasper says to me. "We have to be missing something with Ivor. There has to be more to this story."

I totally agree with Jasper. I have been mulling it over, and it just doesn't add up. Why would Ivor be going to all this trouble over a broken heart? Why target Ellie? There are literally millions of human women out there. Any of them would be an easier target than Ellie.

"Do you have any theories?" I ask.

"Nothing solid," Jasper says. "But I think I'm going to make some calls while we are heading back to the office. We need to know more about why Ivor would have chosen to turn a human instead of finding a 'strong, thick-blooded woman' in his own pack. It just doesn't feel right. You know?"

"You're right," I say. "Everything we know about him, Olf, and the Iceland pack tells me that he would never pick a human woman. It makes a nice story, but it's full of holes. I feel like we are being sold some bullshit here."

Ivor has kept us so busy tracking him that we haven't really had time to dissect his motives. Now that we are sure he is here, we've identified his next target, and we have time to think about why he is doing all of this, nothing is adding up.

"I'll talk to Ellie more about her conversation with Anna, too," I say. "She may have some information that can help us figure this out. Anna said he was mumbling about a true wolf king and 'the one,' so maybe that's a start."

Jasper spends the whole ride back to the office talking to his people in the archives department and pack relations. He hopes to gain some insight into why Ivor would have started a relationship with a human woman.

Pulling up to the office, I nod to the PS members stationed outside. There are two visible out front and one that I can see prowling the roof. I'm sure there are more on the other sides of the building as well. I feel confident that Ivor can't get to Ellie as long as she stays here.

While we were gone, Ellie called Candy into the office to meet with us. We all need to be a part of this plan to identify our pack mole and finish Ivor.

When we step out of the elevator, I can smell her, and it brings an involuntary smile to my face. When I look around, I can see Candy staring at me, smirking. Walking over to her, I put an arm around her and pull her in for a bear hug.

"What are you smirking at?" I ask.

Candy squeezes me and whispers, "I saw that look on your face when you caught her scent coming off the elevator. You aren't fooling anyone, boy, least of all this old bat."

I shake my head and smile at my aunt.

"I have no idea what you are talking about," I say. "I am just relieved that she is still here and hasn't wandered off with a killer again. Speaking of, why don't you ask her to join us in the conference room, and we can start discussing our next moves."

Candy grabs my hand in hers and looks me dead in my eyes. Quietly, she whispers, "Bo, I know the look of true love. I've seen it on the faces of Roman and your father, and many others. I know that shine in your eyes when you scent her, and I can see the weight that lifts off your shoulders when she is nearby. Human or not, that girl is deep in your soul. You need to be careful or you're going to end up with a broken heart, kiddo."

I am momentarily stunned by Candy's words.

"You don't need to worry about me," I say with as much false confidence as I can muster. "I am just protective of the first human government official to come live amongst us. It's super important for all of us that this arrangement with the U.S. government goes smoothly."

Candy looks a little disappointed at my declaration. Shaking her head, she drops my hand and heads toward my office to collect Ellie.

We have a lot to cover in our meeting. Ellie texted me earlier to let me know that she has some ideas about catching our mole. Jasper has been on the phone with his German scholars, and based on his body language, he isn't super happy with what he is hearing. Hopefully, it's something that helps us identify Ivor's true motives.

Roman, Chester, Candy, Ellie, and I bustle around the conference room. Janeal has dropped off several trays of food for us and the Squad members protecting the building. We all make ourselves plates while we wait for Jasper to join us so that we can start the meeting.

I take the time to explain our theory to the others that Ivor has some other motivation, aside from the heartbreak story we have been fed. Glancing at Ellie, I see that she looks deep in thought.

"Ellie," I say. "Anna told you that Ivor started talking crazy when she rejected his wolf, right? Did she mention anything else other than 'True King' and 'the one?'"

Ellie looks up and smiles. "We can review it together," she says. "I recorded the call just in case we needed to go back to it for evidence or clues."

My eyes light up, and a smile breaks my face in two. This woman is amazing. Of course, she recorded the call.

Ellie scoots back to my office and returns with her laptop. In a few moments, she connects it to the large screen in the conference room. By the time she is ready, Jasper is joining us.

"Ellie recorded her conversation with Anna," I say to him when he sits at the table. "We were just waiting for you before we play it back. Hopefully, it gives us some new clues about Ivor's true motives here."

Jasper sits and places his phone on the table. He looks up at Ellie with a stern expression and nods in approval, "Smart."

Everyone looks concerned, and for good reason. It takes an act of Luna to knock the playfulness out of Jasper. I'm not sure that I have ever seen him act so seriously. I've certainly never heard him give a single-word answer before. Jasper loves the sound of his own voice.

Ellie looks at him with a frown. She and Jasper have become fast friends, and I know that she is worried about him as well. There is a tiny pang of jealousy in the depths of my chest. It makes me wonder if, given the choice, she would run off and live with Jasper. Of course, that is ridiculous, isn't it? I mean, they have grown to tease and mock each other like siblings…or is that flirting?

Before I start to spiral too hard, Ellie starts the recording of her video call with Anna. Everyone in the room gasps.

"Holy shit Ellie," Jasper says loudly. "She could be your fucking twin sister."

Jasper stands from the table so abruptly that his chair flies backward. While we are all struck by how much Anna and Ellie look alike, Jasper seems unusually upset by it, and we all look at him, stunned.

"Jay, what the hell is going on?" I ask.

Jasper starts to pace as he gathers his thoughts to reply.

"One of the theories that my research team floated to me was that Ivor may be looking for the latest human reincarnation of Datura, the lost daughter of Luna," he says. "The one from the stories your mom used to tell us as kids."

"You can't be serious," Roman chimes in.

Everyone around the table gasps, and their faces give away their surprise at the idea.

"Ok," Ellie says. "So, talk to me like I have no idea about any of this, you know, because I don't."

Finally, Jasper gives Ellie a wink and a weak smile. "There is an old bedtime story, it was Bo's favorite. Anyway, some of our people believe that the story is actually a prophecy. It claims that the Goddess Luna sent her daughter, Datura, to live amongst the hybrids, which would be us, and learn about us. Luna wanted to know if we were worthy of the Ulfheðnar's gift. Jehovah, the God of humans, and Luna's brother, took offense at her questioning the worthiness of his children. Jehovah found Datura, erased her memories, and cursed her. Essentially trapping her in this realm as a normal human woman with no access to her wolf. The story claims that the True King of the wolf walkers would find Datura and restore her wolf blood, releasing her from Jehovah's hold."

Ellie's face is soft and almost childlike as she listens to the story of Datura. I can imagine her telling the story to her own daughter one day. A tiny, chubby version of Ellie, with big, bright eyes and soft blonde hair. The thought makes me happy and sad, and angry all at once. It's very confusing.

I give myself an internal shake. I need to focus.

"What makes you think this is tied to Ellie?" I ask. "That story is one of hundreds of fables."

"It's the look," Jasper says. "Apparently, in the original, extended version of the story, there is a description of Datura. She is said to have been built by the Goddess to blend into the human world perfectly. The only defining characteristics being her golden hair and hybrid-like build."

All eyes turn to Ellie. Her strong build is something everyone notices, Jasper even joked that she looked like a wolf.

"It's funny," Ellie says. "I've always thought of myself as designed by the Gods to blend in. I never thought a plain Jane look would make me a target for a lunatic. Guess I should have spent more time watching makeup videos and learning how to make myself stand out."

Jasper is pacing again. "Think about it, Bo. All the victims were active women. All of them had varying degrees of blonde hair. We have been assuming that he spent a lot of time with them so that he could torture them or play out some sick fantasy. What if he was testing to see if they were the real Datura?"

"It's not a great theory, but it's the strongest one we've gotten so far," I say. "As crazy as it is, it fits better than an Icelandic alpha going crazy from a broken heart over a human woman."

"It's not just that," Jasper says. "There are some other things that I want us to consider as well. Ellie, what did your parents do before you were born?"

Ellie makes a confused face, but answers. "They were both corporate lawyers."

"Where are you going with this Jay?" I ask.

"Just indulge me for a moment," he says. "Your parents go from corporate lawyers to devoted civil servants. A wolf leader opens up to you about the community he protects with his life. The first thing Bo did was introduce you to his inner circle. The next thing he did was present our children, the most vulnerable citizens we have. Think about it. Throughout your entire career, everywhere you went, peace followed."

This time, it's Ellie who jumps to her feet, eyebrows pinched together tightly. "Excuse me, are you insinuating that my success as a diplomat was because of some divine intervention? Are you kidding me? Because, of course, a woman can't get results unless it's some kind of miracle, right? I worked my ass off for those peace deals."

I turn to Ellie and say, "Whoa, hold on, I don't think Jasper meant it like that. Right?"

"Luna, no," Jasper says, holding up his hands in surrender. "Ellie, please, just hear me out. That's not what I'm saying at all."

Ellie crosses her arms and stares at Jasper with an intensity that I swear has a physical presence in the room. I never want to be on the other end of that look.

Jasper takes a deep breath and continues. "I just mean, Ellie, that your light is so bright that it inspires others to be better. Your intentions are so damn pure, that people *want* to live up to your vision of them. You might not see it, sweetheart, but you *are* something special. We all knew it the first time we met you, and it just makes me wonder if Ivor might be right about you."

Ellie relaxes her gaze and unfurls her arms. Cracking a half smile, she gives Jasper the 'I'm watching you' two-finger point. "I'm going to let you slide, this time. Mostly because you said I'm special enough to be a Goddess."

I'm not sure I can handle much more of this.

"Let's just watch the Anna video and see what else we can learn from that," I say, sighing heavily.

We watch the video of the conversation, and much of what Anna says about Ivor's rantings after she refused him seems to line up with Jasper's theory about Datura.

"I think we need to confront Olf with our new information," I say to the group. "There is no way that he isn't aware of Ivor's true mission. I want to know everything that Olf knows. What do you guys think?"

Roman speaks up first. "I agree, he has clearly been holding back information. My guess is that he believes that Ivor will find Datura and somehow leverage her to take control over all the packs."

Chester chimes in next. "I agree too. I'd like to suggest that Roman and I fly there with a few kittens and speak with Olf in person. Asking kindly hasn't worked with him so far. It's time we remind him of who we are."

Jasper agrees and adds his own men into the equation. "The time has come to show Olf and his pack where they stand. I've let them slide on a lot because they are small and they are the root of our lineage, but they have gone too far now."

It takes a lot for Jasper to throw his weight as the leader of all the packs around. He doesn't believe in a monarchy, and he certainly doesn't want to interfere in anyone else's pack business.

"Olf will cooperate with you, Chester," Jasper continues, "or he'll face *my* consequences. Aside from the fact that Ivor is killing humans and putting us all at risk, Ellie is a member of this pack, and is therefore, ultimately, under my protection. It will be known across all the packs; I will not tolerate any pack intentionally targeting another."

Jasper's words come out so cold that I swear he actually lowered the temperature of the room. We are all quiet for a moment. It's easy to forget that Jasper is the most dominant alpha in the realm. He is so friendly and easygoing, always laughing, and making jokes, but not now, not today. Today, Jasper takes his role very seriously and Luna help Olf and the Icelandic pack if they cross him.

"We still have one more unpleasant issue to discuss," I say to the group. It's no use dancing around it. "We have a mole. Someone from inside the pack is feeding Ivor information, and we need to find out who it is."

Candy is the first to speak, "Are you sure, Bo? I just can't imagine someone in our circle feeding information to Ivor."

"I know," I reply. "But there really isn't any other explanation for how he was able to find Ellie so fast. How he knew where my house was, and when Ellie would be alone, what to say to get her to leave with him, and where her new home is."

Ellie chimes in next, "I have an idea to figure out who the mole is. We use the old high school rumor trick."

We all look at each other, dumbfounded. "Ok," I say, "Now you need to talk to us like we have no idea what you are talking about."

"Really," Ellie says, looking at each of our faces. "You guys never had someone in high school spread rumors about you, so you tell all your friends a different story to see which one gets circulated, and then you know who the rat is."

We are all stunned. "No," I say. "I was the alpha's son, so I went to a special school. If someone talked bad about you, we just fought."

"Well," Ellie says, "Score one for camp human, then. The plan is simple: You make up a couple of stories about how Ivor can get to me. We plant those stories with different people. Whichever one he follows up on, that person is our mole."

The plan is both simple and brilliant. We throw out a few lies and see which one floats to the surface. None of us are happy about lying to our loved ones, but we all know what is at stake here.

We decide to go with a story about secretly flying Ellie out of the pack lands for her safety. We give each suspect a different day on which we will fly her out. Chester will tell his girlfriend that we fly on Monday, Jasper will tell my mother we fly on Tuesday, Ellie will tell Janeal we fly on Wednesday, and Roman will tell Francine we fly on Thursday.

The plan is to tell each suspect that the other days are decoys, and that Ellie will only actually move with the convoy on one of them.

I flat-out refused to let Ellie ride with us to the airport, but she insisted, and the others agreed with her—even Jasper. *Traitor.*

"If Ivor doesn't smell her unique scent," Candy says, "Then he'll know it's a trap."

Jasper added, "Ivor won't be expecting a trap; he'll assume that he has the element of surprise. We'll use some Fae charms to hide our scents from him. He'll think it is just the two of you. But really, it'll be a group of us."

With the plan in motion, the only thing we can do now is wait. We'll have to wait for Chester and Roman to return with news from Olf, and then we'll have to wait to see who the mole is. Wait, wait, and wait. We have about a week to gather as much information as we can.

Chapter Twenty-Five

Roman and Chester have landed in Iceland and met up with Jasper's men. According to Roman, Jasper did not play around with his choices for deployed soldiers.

"By Luna, son," Roman says. "These lads make me feel small as a newborn pup. What is he feeding these boys over there?"

I can't help but laugh. Roman is a descendant of the wolf-bear line. They are known as some of the largest and strongest wolfmen to ever have walked this realm. If Roman is feeling small, that means that Jasper sent the largest and most intimidating men in his pack to greet Olf.

"I think Olf may have hit a nerve with Jasper," I say to Roman. "He's pretty pissed. I don't think I've seen him this mad since he caught that guy wolfbaning girls in college."

"I'm telling you, lad," The old man continues. "These fellas scared the bejesus out of the airport staff. They are all very German. You know the type. Stern face, razor-sharp features, fierce eyes. Olf has no idea what he's in for."

I agree with Roman that we're showing an overwhelming presence, especially with Jasper's elite squad behind us, but I don't want to underestimate Olf either. We don't know how long this plan has been in motion or how deep it goes.

"Just be careful, Old Man," I say. "For all we know, Olf has his entire pack ready for war."

I can hear Chester in the background grilling one of Jasper's men about how much he can lift. The elite German force must think we are a bunch of loons. I just pray to Luna that they don't have to see what Chester and Roman are really made of during this trip.

Roman promises to update us as soon as his meeting with Olf is over. I turn my attention to planning our trap.

Jasper, Ellie, and I slip into my office. We have another part of the mole investigation to discuss, and it requires total privacy.

When we are all settled, I start us off.

"We have to address the very unlikely and, frankly, disgusting elephant in the room," I say. "There is a possibility that the mole isn't any of our suspects and is instead one of my advisors. The only way to know for sure is to wait and see if Ivor doesn't attack at all. There is no way he'll let Ellie leave now that he is so close."

"Shit," Jasper says. "You're right, if Ivor doesn't attack, then it's because he knows it's a trap and that Ellie was never actually leaving."

Ellie picks up Jasper's train of thought, "And if he knows it's a trap, that means that someone tipped him off to it. But why would someone who knows me, and who loves you guys, do that?"

"I don't know," I say, reluctantly. "It's part of what makes all of this so hard to combat. We don't know the motives of the mole. Do they believe, like Ivor, in Datura? Do they hate humans? Do they just want to hurt me? Are they trying to weaken the pack? Without understanding why someone would betray us, I can't narrow down who it is any more than we have so far."

※

Ellie connects her laptop to the screen in the conference room. Roman and Chester have video-called us from Iceland with their update.

With a flicker of the big screen, we can all see and talk to Roman and Chester.

"Hey boys," Jasper says in his much more normal chipper tone. "How'd it go?"

Roman smiles while Chester lets out a full belly laugh.

Roman answers, "Well, we marched straight through the town center to the town hall and demanded to be seen. When they wouldn't let us in, I kicked the doors down."

Ellie puts a hand to her mouth.

Roman continues, "I'm so sorry, sweet Ellie. We are beyond normal diplomatic procedures now and solidly in the land of kill or be killed. Anyway, Olf tried to put up a good show, but he was overwhelmed by our force, thanks to Jasper's unnaturally large boys. We allowed him to empty the town hall and speak with us privately, and he absolutely spilled his guts."

I lean forward in my chair, "Tell us everything."

Roman tells us the story he got from Olf. Apparently, the brothers have been researching the legend of Datura for years. They cooked up the idea after a member of their pack found a new cave near the original Ulfheðnar portal that contained drawings that Olf and Ivor believed to be the story of Datura. They believe that the cave drawings prove that the fable is actually true.

Ivor believed that if he were to find Datura and restore her wolf, she would crown him the true king of the wolves and help him rule over all of the packs. However, he couldn't really find anything to tell him how to identify the goddess in her human form.

The only thing they had to go on was a vague description of a blonde woman with wolf-like features, but not actually a wolf. He also found information that suggested she would smell of a clean soul. Ivor thought that the woman would be in Iceland since that was the original land that the Ulfheðnar roamed.

After searching villages all over, he decided that Anna had to be Datura. She was not scared of him and easily accepted his proposal to be his wife. Her scent also carried a fresh air smell to it. But, once he offered to turn her into a wolf and she refused, he determined that she couldn't be Datura.

While Ivor was off with Anna, Olf made a discovery. The last piece of the puzzle fell into place when Olf and his scholars found a mention of the "noble wolf king" being the one to restore Datura's wolf form and memories.

"Oh, my goodness," Ellie gasps. "He thinks it's Jasper. Adolpha is noble wolf."

"What," Jasper says looking between all of us. "How do you know that; how does she know that?"

Roman laughs, "It's her hidden talent, boy. Anyway, hearing this news, Ivor went to Germany next, believing that Jasper must have Datura there already. He identified a few women he thought could be Datura, but after giving them his blood, he found that they had only been human. Then he killed them."

Chester picks up the story, "Next, he traveled to the United States to seek out more potential Daturas. But none of them panned out. He was getting desperate and sloppy until he heard of Ellie. Her scent and build made her a prime candidate. Not to mention her close proximity to the Noble Wolf King himself."

Jasper mockingly puffs up his chest in a sad attempt to look royal and noble.

"Roman," I say when Jasper is through being an idiot. "Did Olf give you any information about a mole in our pack?"

Roman shakes his head and lowers his face. "He did. He says that Ivor planted a mole in our pack years before they hatched the Datura plan. He knows it is a woman, but that is all. The plan was for her to come to our pack, blend in as if she had always been here, and then attempt to seduce you. Ivor wanted her to marry you, kill you, marry him, and then hand him your pack."

Chester chimes in, "Bo, I don't know much about Ember. She's Celia's friend, but I'm not even sure how long they've known each other. I'm really sorry. I really didn't have any reason to believe that she was anything but a nice girl who might make you happy."

I shake my head and hold up my hand. "Please, Chester, don't apologize. We don't even know if Ember is the mole. Let's not jump to any conclusions here. For all we know, the mole could be someone completely off our radar."

"Bo's right," Ellie adds. "We don't know who the mole is, and it won't help anything to assume or accuse anyone without proof. We have a plan in place to figure it out, and we will wait until then to start thinking about how this happened."

Chapter Twenty-Six

Monday comes, and we are all on edge. It's day one of our plan to catch Ivor and identify our mole. If Ivor attacks today, we know it is Ember, and that she is getting her information from Chester's girlfriend.

Ellie and I wait out front of the office for a PS member to bring an SUV for us. Ellie is disguised so that an onlooker won't know if it is really her or a decoy. The plan is that she and I will enter the SUV alone together in front of the office for anyone to see. This way, if anyone is watching us, they will think that it is simply the two of us in the truck together.

Of course, Jasper and three PS members were hidden inside the vehicle before it reached the street.

We climb into the truck and start our drive.

"I'm so nervous I feel like I'm going to puke," Ellie says looking at me with a forced smile.

I reach over the center console and squeeze her hand. "Don't worry," I say. "We have enough men and firepower in this truck to take down a SWAT team, Ivor doesn't stand a chance."

Jasper laughs from the back of the SUV. "You know," he says. "Now that you two have some alone time, feel free to discuss your relationship, in great detail."

Ellie laughs, and I can feel a little of the tension leaving her. As much as I want to curse Jasper out, his inappropriate humor is helping Ellie to relax.

"Ok," I say. "So, Ellie, now that we are alone, I'm really curious how you feel about the new sustainable asphalt alternative. Do you think it's worth the cost increase? And what about that proposal for redistricting the schools?"

Jasper lets out an exaggerated sigh. "You suck, we want the good stuff. For instance, Ellie, how do you feel knowing that Ivor believes you're a reincarnated wolf goddess?"

Ellie and I only talked briefly about the Datura story, and, honestly, I'm not mad about Jasper bringing it up. I do wish that we were actually alone, but that hasn't been an easy feat since we discovered that Ivor was after Ellie.

Ellie looks like she is deep in thought. It takes her a few moments to reply.

"I've been thinking about it a lot," she says. "I mean, who is to say if the story is real or not? I would have never believed it a year ago, but I also wouldn't have believed that werewolves were real either. I mean, I don't *think* that I am the reincarnation of Datura, but how would I know?"

"I guess you wouldn't know," I say. "But that doesn't really answer the question. If we figure out a way to test the theory, would you want to know if you are Datura?"

"I'm not sure," Ellie says. "I mean, I've never been anything but a plain Jane. What would it even mean to be the daughter of Luna? A goddess? What is the expectation for Datura? Would she be made to leave Earth and go back to the divine realm? Is she supposed to stay? I mean, she was sent here to live among the wolf hybrids and learn about them, but we don't really know why. And, if Luna is watching over the Ulfheðnar and Jehovah is watching over the humans, is Datura here to watch over the hybrids?"

"That's a good point," Jasper says. "If we find out that you *are* Datura, will you be forced to leave us? I hadn't thought about that."

I can feel the tightening in my jaw. I don't like the thought of Ellie being ripped away from us to live in a realm that she didn't even know existed six months ago. We've only just found each other. There is still so much I want to show her and teach her about our world.

There really is no denying that Ellie is important to me. In the short time that I've gotten to know her, she has grown into a major staple in my life. I can't bear to lose her, not in a way where I could never get her back.

What could I do? It's one thing to keep her safe from Ivor. It's a whole other thing to try to deny Luna access to her own daughter. Her daughter who is also a freaking goddess.

There's no way that fate could be this cruel. To send Ellie into my life, into all our lives, just to rip her away and send her to the Divine realm. No mortal being can go there, and I'm sure Luna would never allow her daughter to return to Earth. We would be cut off from Ellie forever.

Would Ellie even remember us? If she really is Datura, and her memories are restored, what happens to Ellie's memories?

I'm in a shit mood for the rest of the drive. But we make it to the airport, and then we board the plane without incident. It looks like Monday is a bust.

We returned to the SUV and start heading back to the office. We'll exit the SUV in the underground parking so that nobody can see that Ellie has returned with me or the hidden men inside the SUV with us.

We scheduled our strongest suspicion for Monday. It looks like Chester can breathe a sigh of relief. Of course, just because Chester's girlfriend isn't the leak doesn't mean that Ember isn't the mole.

Tomorrow will be Ember's second try. We will repeat the same pattern as today, but hopefully with better conversation. Talking about Ellie being turned into a wolf and then possibly leaving us was not exactly my idea of pleasant small talk.

Jasper and I sneak Ellie back into the office building. As a precaution, we stationed PS members on the street to see if they could notice her. None of them were able to spot her, so if Ivor or his mole were watching, they wouldn't notice anything different.

When we enter the conference room, I'm shocked to see new food on the table. I look to Roman and ask where it came from.

Apparently, Janeal insisted on bringing food, and while there, she also insisted on seeing Ellie.

Luckily, Roman was able to explain to her that Ellie was in hiding and that even she would not be allowed to see Ellie—not without my express consent. Janeal countered, telling Roman that she was "wink, wink in on it" and that she promised not to tell anyone.

Roman, of course, still denied her. He explained to her that I would have his head if I found out he had let anyone see Ellie. However, for good measure, Roman did ask Janeal to bring Ellie some new clothes from the house tomorrow. He gave her the same "wink, wink."

I thank Roman. The old boy is quick on his feet. If Janeal is our mole, as unlikely as that could be, he did a good job of persuading her that Ellie really was in hiding.

Furthermore, when we get to the central office where Ellie really is hiding, we see that her gym bag is near the front of the door with a fan blowing on it. I raise my eyebrows at Roman.

"What? The kittens let me know that Janeal was on her way up here," he says to me. "I had ample time to set up a scent for her to solidify my story that Ellie was still here."

Shaking my head at the old man, I genuinely smile for the first time all day.

"I'm sure as hell glad you're on our side, Roman," I say to him.

Ellie runs up to him and gives him a big old bear hug. "Thank you, Roman," she says to him. "I know it's not easy for you to lie to your own people on behalf of a human."

Roman hugs Ellie tightly for a moment, then pulls her to arm's length and looks her dead in her eyes. "Sweet Ellie, it is my honor and my privilege to protect you. You are one of us. It doesn't matter that you are not wolf born, you are wolf in heart. "

Hearing Roman say that Ellie is a wolf at heart makes my mood sour again.

As much as I want to dismiss the Datura story as an old wives' tale, a Cinderella-type story for wolves, something in my chest won't let me let go. I have that same feeling now as I did the first time that I thought that Ivor could be going after Ellie.

I decide to follow my intuition this time. I ask Ellie if we can talk privately for a while.

The two of us enter the central office and close the door behind us. We are sure to sit away from the door, and we use hushed tones as we speak. I need this conversation to be private between Ellie and me only.

"You're right," I say to her. "This isn't some cheesy romance novel, and we have a lot on our plates right now with Ivor, but I just can't ignore these feelings anymore."

※

We only leave the central office to retrieve food and more water. I don't care about the whispers. Ellie and I remain sequestered in the central office together for the entire night.

When we finally emerge from the office around mid-morning the next day, the time has come to play our little game again. We repeat the exact same process as the previous day.

This time, Ellie controls the conversation in the car on the way to the airport. She tells stories of growing up with diplomats for parents. She regales my PS members with stories from around the world. She talks about how hard it was to leave her childhood friends every few years. She talks about how it created a bit of a hole in her. Ellie tells the sad story of how she's never really gotten close to anyone since she was a child. The men listen to her tales as if she is an alien from a distant planet. All these men have grown up in a close community surrounded by family. The idea of being so alone is completely foreign to them.

While I'm grateful that Ellie is controlling the conversation, Luna knows I didn't want to answer any questions about our night together, it makes me incredibly sad to hear Ellie speak about her life alone. How could such an incredible and loving woman be denied the bond of community, family, and love?

I'm so lost in Ellie's stories that I almost miss the car pulled off to the side of the road ahead of us.

"Look alive, boys," I call out to the back. "We have a car on the side of the road ahead. I am going to stop and see if we can help out. If Ember is our mole, then this could be our trap."

The men grunt in acknowledgment. I slow down as we approach the car. The front tire seems to be flat and there is a person inside the car. It looks like a woman, but the glare of the windshield makes it hard to see inside.

I motion for Ellie to duck down into the floor area.

As we approach the car, I lower my window about halfway. I don't want whoever is looking into our SUV to have a clear view.

I can see the front window of the car beginning to lower as we inch closer. A young girl sticks her face out the window and smiles at me as she waves her left hand in a friendly greeting.

"Are you OK?" I yell to the car.

The girl looks at me with a bit of shock, then puts her hand to her face. "Oh, my Luna," she says. "You're the alpha, right, Bo? I'm so sorry to bother you. I got a flat."

I smile as warmly as I can, I'm on full alert, but I don't want to tip my hand if this really is our trap.

With a small laugh, I reply, "Yes, I'm Bo. Are you OK? Do you need a hand, or do you want me to call someone for you? It's pretty remote out here."

The girl shakes her head in small, quick movements. "No, sir, um, I'm fine. It was stupid, really. I wasn't really paying attention to the road, and I guess I hit something. But it's fine, really. I'm so sorry,

I'm so embarrassed. My dad and brother are on their way. I'm fine, really. I don't need to bother you with this."

I smile at her broadly. I don't detect any deceit from her. "How far away are your father and brother? I can wait with you until they get here."

"No, sir, really. They should be here any second. They both work at the airstrip, and I just was delivering lunch to them," she says.

Again, I don't detect any deceit from the girl. As we are chatting, I can hear a car in the distance. Sure enough, her father and brother drive up to us in a few moments' time.

When her father emerges from the car, I instantly recognize him as one of our airfield mechanics.

"Rowan," I say when the man is close enough, "No way this is your daughter. Has it really been that long since I've seen her that she's a young woman now?"

My long-time employee smiles and nods his head. "I'm afraid so, Bo. It appears that we might be getting old."

"Hey," I say back with mock indignation. "Speak for yourself, old man. I'll let you guys get to it then. Take your time. There will be no flights today."

We drive off from the scene and continue monitoring the surrounding areas as we proceed to the airfield.

Again, we made it to the airfield and board the plane without incident. Day two is a bust. It looks like Ember might not be our mole after all.

That leaves me with a sick feeling in my stomach. Tomorrow, we will test Janeal, and then on Thursday, we will focus on Francine. Neither woman has ever given me a reason to doubt them. But to be honest, I don't know much about their social lives or friends.

If he doesn't attack, does that really mean that one of my advisors is the mole? Roman, Chester, and Candy are as close to me as my own parents. Candy is literally my blood.

Could we be wrong? Is there no mole? Could Ivor have just gotten lucky? Did he research our town ahead of time?

It seems like nothing makes sense anymore.

Chapter Twenty-Seven

Ellie, Jasper, and I decide to eat dinner together in the central office. We are all feeling the pressure of possibly being wrong about a mole. Part of me is relieved at the idea of being wrong; it means no one betrayed us. But the other part is downright sick over it. It would mean that we are once again two steps behind Ivor and that we wrongly accused one of our own people of being a traitor.

 We are seated at a small round table that is practically covered with food tins. Janeal really did go all out for her friend.

"So," Ellie says, breaking the tension. "I think it is reasonable to scratch Ember off the list of suspects."

Jasper and I both nod in agreement.

"Maybe," She continues, "I don't know, maybe Ivor isn't getting help. Or maybe it isn't someone that we ever thought of. Could there be bugs in any of the cars or offices? Maybe even something like cell phone tapping?"

Jasper shakes his head. "I honestly don't know. I mean, he made a fool of us when we should have had the upper hand, but it makes sense that he had help to do that. To tap our phones or bug the cars or offices, he would still have needed help. Plus, Olf confirmed that Ivor sent a plant to Bo's pack. The simple fact that he thought Bo would get married is proof that he isn't smart enough to pull this off without help."

"What the hell is that supposed to mean?" I ask.

Ellie lets out a tiny giggle. "Janeal did tell me that you never date, and when you do, it never lasts long. She also warned me about you not being great husband material."

I look between Jasper and Ellie, "Are you two working for my mother now? Sheesh, attacked. So I have high standards, is that a crime? And I'll have you know that I'm great husband material."

"Ok," Jasper says. "Spill it."

"Spill what?" I ask.

"You know what," Jasper says, looking between me and Ellie. "What's going on between you two?"

Ellie's face turns beet red. I look at Jasper with my best 'seriously' face.

"Come on," Jasper says. "We are all adults here. Everyone knows you two have a connection; a blind man could see it. Then you cozy up all night in Bo's office, so come on, spill it. What's going on? Should I be celebrating with you guys, or are we still tiptoeing around the obvious?"

"Oh. My. Luna," I say, running my hand over my face. "Is this really necessary? We are in the middle of trying to track and catch a psychotic rogue alpha. Don't we have more important things to focus on right now?"

Jasper raises his eyebrows at me, "Absolutely not. There is nothing more important to me right now than this. You are my brother, and Ellie is, well, honestly, she's probably way too good for you, but if she has agreed to lower herself down to you, I want to celebrate that with you guys. I need some positivity in my life, man."

I look over at Ellie, I need some direction here. She shrugs her shoulders at me and throws her hands up.

"Fine," I say, letting out a long sigh. "We spent the night talking, mostly. We decided that we would see where things go organically. We aren't going to put a lot of pressure on each other to define things or plan the future too much. Right now, we are living in the moment.

There are a lot of things that we haven't figured out yet. And, most importantly, we are not going public."

"I knew it," Jasper says, pumping his fist in the air. "But what the hell, I'm not 'the public.' You could have told me."

Ellie saves me, "It's not like we've had a lot of time to talk. We weren't trying to hide anything from you, we just didn't get the chance to tell you yet. We thought it would be better to wait until everything with Ivor was settled before we tried to talk about it. But you're so damn nosy."

"For the love of Luna," I say. "Do *not* tell my mother."

"Fine," Jasper agrees, "but you have to keep her off my back about settling down."

"I'm serious Jay," I say. "We can't let this get out yet. There are too many considerations. Pack law and treaty laws, not to mention potential challenges to Ellie for her position. Ellie and I need time to figure out what this is and work through all the complications together before we face the world. This could ruin Ellie's life if it gets out before we're ready for it."

Jasper looks between the two of us with a serious expression. "I understand the risks, Bo. I would never do anything to hurt you guys. I'm just excited to finally see you making a move and grabbing for happiness."

Ellie puts her hand on Jasper's shoulder, "I know you're on our side with this. Bo's just scared that the pack won't accept a human, and he doesn't want to see his community crumble because of his choices. We just need to take it slow and watch our steps."

"I get it," Jasper says. "But I'm the high alpha, and you have my support. We can handle any fallout together. I'll stand behind you 100%, but you need to promise me, Bo, that you aren't just going to focus on all the reasons you shouldn't be together. I know better than most that everything can change in the blink of an eye. Don't sacrifice a second of happiness because you're afraid of what other people think."

Jasper rarely talks about losing his family, but I know that it had a big impact on the way he lives his life. He changed afterward, becoming more of a thrill seeker, spending more time traveling, and even calling and visiting me more.

I nod to him. "I promise, Jay. I won't let fear of what could go wrong keep me from what might go right. I'm following the 'what would Jasper do' method."

"For the love of Luna," Jasper says with a laugh. "Don't ever do that!"

I look over at Ellie and she smiles sweetly. I guess we are really doing this. My mother is going to lose her mind.

"So," Jasper interrupts my thoughts, "Whatever happened with your message to Ember? Did she answer you?"

"What message?" Ellie asks.

"Bo sent her a breakup text," Jasper says.

"You did not break up with her over text!" Ellie scolds me.

"No," I say defensively. "You have to be dating someone to break up with them. To be honest, I never got around to reading her reply. We've been kinda busy."

I open my text thread with Ember and stare at the message. A huff of laughter escapes me.

"You guys aren't going to believe this," I say, sliding my phone over towards Jasper.

> *Oh thank Luna you aren't interested. To be honest, at first, I thought you were gay too and that your mother was trying to set up a lavender marriage between us. I figured I'd take one for the team and the good of the pack, but then I realized you were straight and I was too scared to tell your*

*mother that I'm a lesbian. Please don't
tell anyone. I'm not fully out to my family.*

Jasper and Ellie both burst out laughing.

Between laughs, Jasper says, "We could have saved ourselves two
days' work if you had just manned up and spoken to her."

I snatch back my phone and type out a quick message to Ember:

*Why did Celia try to set us up in the
first place?*

I guess she didn't realize I was gay.

I thought you two were friends??

We met because I was hitting on her.

Guess she didn't realize.

Well, your secret is safe with me!

*Thanks. I'll tell your mom we went
out if you want.*

*Thanks, I could use a break from
her matchmaking!*

PART THREE:

Ivor

Chapter Twenty-Eight

Today is the day. Finally. That pretty-boy thin-blooded German will finally get what is coming to him. I will free Datura, and the Moon Goddess will reward me with the title of True King.

Once I am in charge of all the packs, I can ditch the clingy bitch wolf and marry a strong female. Maybe the Moon Goddess will grant me her daughter as a wife. That would be perfect. No one would dare challenge our reign with the blood of the Goddess running through the veins of my sons.

"Ivor, my love," she calls to me from her kitchen. She has been in this lowly pack for too long. She has become as soft and weak as the rest of them. At this point, I'm not even sure she'll be able to handle the human woman.

Originally, I sent her to this pack to seduce their alpha, Bo. I figured that he would be looking for a wife, so I sent him the perfect package. Once he married her, she would be my insider and help me take over the pack as their new alpha.

With this pack's size and my pack's strength, we would take down Jasper and his pack with ease. Then, not even Olf would dare stand against me.

But she failed me.

At first, she claimed her failure was because Bo was not interested in women. She claimed that he shunned every woman his mother pushed at him. Then she blamed the human. Apparently, Bo took an instant liking to her.

It is my fault, really; I should never have trusted a woman with such a task. She was too weak of mind to see how important this step was in the plan. All she could focus on was becoming my wife and living the life of a queen. She couldn't wait to be a pampered woman.

That is why she could not seduce Bo. He is an alpha, with alpha senses. There is no way that he would fall for someone who is focusing her attention on another man. Greedy bitch couldn't put her own desires aside for the mission.

But no matter, I am here now, and I am closer than ever to getting what I deserve.

Finding Datura is even better than taking the packs by force. Olf and I have always dreamed of being the ones to locate the missing daughter of Luna.

We studied the story as children and dreamed of the day when we would be crowned the True Kings.

Of course, that was childish nonsense. There could only ever be one King, and it *will* be me. That is why I never challenged my brother for leadership of our pack. I needed to be able to work in the shadows on my own plans. I didn't have time to deal with politics and petty squabbles.

It is my destiny to find the lost goddess and claim the crown. How else can you explain the way she was practically presented right to me? An alpha who shuns every strong female wolf takes an immediate liking to a stupid human. Then, that human walks right into the clutches of my woman. It was almost too easy.

"Ivvvooooorrr," she whines, like a child. "Come out here and eat your breakfast before it gets cold."

I turn from the window and begin the short walk to the kitchen. Her home is small, but at least she is away from the center of their ridiculous city. It has been easy to hide here. I planted old clothing all over the woods and have used very strong animal scents to mask my presence. Besides, she is a trusted member of the community. If she had noticed anyone around her property, surely, she would have called the aptly named "kitten" squad.

What self-respecting wolf would allow such a name?

"Let us review the plan," I say when I reach the table.

"I know the plan," she says while rolling her eyes. She has definitely been in this pack for far too long. Maybe I'll kill her when this is over. She is likely too weak to make for a good servant, and Luna knows I won't be marrying her. I refuse to allow weak pups in my pack, especially of my own blood.

"This is important, woman!" I say. "You must follow the plan exactly. You cannot fail. If we don't get the human away from them in one piece, all will be lost."

She looks at me and points to the food. "I understand," she says. "I know how important it is. I also know that Bo and Jasper are strong, and you need to eat to be at your best."

I sit in front of the food and begin eating while gesturing for her to keep talking and tell me the plan from her memory.

"You will shoot the tires from Bo's SUV right where we shot that young girl's tire out. When they stop to investigate, you run at Bo and Jasper first. I will wait to hear the signal from you and drive up to the fight. I yell to Ellie to get into my car quickly so that I can drive her to safety. I knock her out, tie her up, and put her in my trunk. Then, I wait for you at the meeting point near Ellie's home," she says, throwing her hands in the air. "Happy?"

"Yes,' I say between bites. "Do not fail me. Get the girl at all costs. You must get her away from Bo and Jasper. She is the key."

"She's not that special," the stupid, jealous woman says in her child-like whining tone. "We don't need her to take the pack. You can submit Bo without her."

Her jealousy makes her weak. If she knew just how important the human is to me, she would have killed her weeks ago and ruined everything. Luckily, her greed makes her easy to control. A promise to her, to be my Queen, is all it took for her to blindly follow my orders.

"You will get her out of there safely," I say sternly. "You will bring her to me, and I will deal with her. If you damage her, I will not be able to use her to get what I need to take down Bo and Jasper in one move. If you want to rule the packs as Queen, you must not fail and you must bring her to me alive and unhurt."

Before she can argue, I add, "Remember, this plan is only in motion because you failed the first time. If you had seduced Bo and become the lady of the pack, we would already be the King and Queen."

With a huff, she lowers her eyes and turns away. I can almost see her tail between her legs. It's a shame there isn't time for me to use her now. When she is submitted like this, it is very attractive. I can't risk it, though. Everything is falling into place, and I won't be derailed by a bitch in heat.

※

We park her car off the road and hide it with branches so the passing SUV won't see it. She'll wait until they drive by, then uncover the car and wait for her queue.

I make my way up to the interception point. I can feel my blood pounding in my veins. This is it, the moment I have been waiting for. I'm so close to getting my hands on Datura. Luna will reward me for freeing her beloved daughter, and I will be the undeniable True King. I'll take Datura for my wife, and together we will rule over this world. We will be giants among ants. The humans will learn their place under our boots. Our kind will grow strong again, and Luna will reward us for proving her to be the superior divine maker.

I set up my rifle and hunker down into my nest of leaves and branches. I will go unseen until it is too late for the foolish, thin-blooded alphas. It is time they learn their place as well.

Chapter Twenty-Nine

The SUV pulls over exactly where I planned. If I had marked the spot with an "X" on the road, they would have parked right on top of it.

I can hear Bo's voice on the breeze.

"Must've hit whatever Rowan's daughter hit the other day," he says to whoever is inside the SUV.

She is here; I can smell her on the breeze as well. I purposefully placed myself downwind of the road so that I would be undetected as I approached them. The time is so close.

Surely, Jasper will emerge from the back seat to assist his friend and watch his back.

Any moment now.

Bo speaks again. "Just stay inside the truck Ellie, this will only take a moment."

Could this dumb shit have really come alone?

Bo climbs into the back seat, and I don't see anyone else in the truck. I can hear him mumbling in there, but I can't make out what he is saying.

A moment later, he is heading to the back of the SUV, where the spare tire has been lowered to the ground from underneath.

I can't believe my luck. I guess I overestimated Bo after all. He must have been so sure of his plan to fool me that he allowed his arrogance to overrule his better judgment. He is here alone with the human.

Then, I hear her sweet voice call out to him. "Is it hard to change a tire? Do you want to call anyone to come help you?"

They are alone.

I start my approach. I will jump him from behind. It may not be the most sporting attack, but in times of war, you do what you must to win. I could have just shot him, but Luna would never reward such cowardice.

I creep up behind him, keeping my cover in the trees and shrubs. I am within jumping distance now.

I leap at his back, but the moment before impact, he slides to the side, and I slam hard into the wheel well of the truck. Just then, the doors fly open, and four more men surround me.

"You did bring backup," I say while sizing up the men around me. I can see Jasper's smug face, and all the rage inside me ignites.

I shift to my wolf form in moments as the men advance on me. I dodge them and leap over one of the guards, catching him with my hide claws in the shoulder.

I spin around, and I can see all five men in front of me now. Bo and Jasper both shift. They are fast shifters and very large wolves. I have never denied that they are strong men, just not as strong as me.

I don't have to kill them all. I just need to pull them away from the car and keep them busy. I can already hear the panic in the human's voice as she shrieks inside the truck.

I let out a loud howl, signaling phase 2 of the plan.

Backing up toward the tree line, I snarl at the wolves in front of me. The three guards will be light work, it is Bo and Jasper that I will need to watch. I lunge at one of the smaller wolves and knock him to the ground easily, but his brothers slam into me almost instantly.

None of them get their teeth into me, though. The wolf that I hit is bleeding from my claws. It isn't a bad wound, but it is a start. I will slowly pick at them, wearing them down. They are soft and pampered, like women and children, compared to the warriors of my pack.

I lunge at the guards one at a time, always getting knocked off them, but always doing just a little more damage to them than they are doing to me.

Bo and Jasper have stayed back; they clearly smell a trap.

I am fighting to get a guard off my back when we all hear it.

A gunshot.

PART FOUR:

Jasper

Chapter Thirty

Bo and I barely spare a glance at each other when we turn to sprint back to the SUV, to Ellie.

When we get to the tree line, there is a second car there. Where the hell is Ellie? We can smell blood in the air, Ellie's blood, and someone else, someone familiar.

Bo and I shift back to human form and start calling her name as we run toward the SUV.

A second shot rings out, and there is a loud thud. Pain rips through my eardrums at the sound. It is so close to us.

We round the back of the SUV, and we see a bleeding wolf slowly starting to shift back to human form. It's Janeal.

"What the FUCK!" Bo yells as he sees his loyal housekeeper and friend struggling to move on the ground.

Turning to Ellie, I can see that she is badly wounded. She is slumped against the rear driver's side tire of the SUV. The gun is still in her hand, but she isn't moving. She is alive, but her wounds don't look good.

It looks like she slammed into the SUV hard when Janeal attacked her. She is bleeding from the back of her head, and her eyes are unfocused.

Bo has grabbed hold of Janeal. He is yelling something, but I am too focused on Ellie to understand it.

Out of the treeline, a large wolf comes into view. It's Ivor. He shifts with alpha speed back to his human form.

He is holding his hands up in surrender as he starts yelling at us to let him save her.

"What the fuck do you mean, save her?" I say, running at him.

I punch him squarely in the jaw, knocking him to the ground. "You did this? Why?"

"She is Datura," he says, moving back to his feet. "She needs thick blood to heal and transform. Janeal was only supposed to bring her to me. That stupid woman can never do anything right. Let me save her and release Datura. I'll be the True King, and she will live by my side. My prize."

I have always had a very strong grip on my wolf form. I can transform faster or slower than any other wolf. I can also control my shifting so that only parts of my body shift at a time. Bo has been able to shift one hand or just his legs, but never in the way that I can.

It isn't something that I show off, and few even know that it can be done.

As Ivor's words leave his mouth, I feel a deep rage inside of me. It's like a burning in the pit of my stomach that spreads heat throughout my whole body. He wants to take my place as leader, Bo's place at Ellie's side, and take over all of our packs. All of this death has been over his ego. His greed for power.

As I move toward this coward of a wolf, who used Janeal and his brother, and that poor human from his village, and killed all those women, I can feel my bones shifting under my skin.

I can feel the muzzle extending from my face. I can feel the fur sprouting from my skin, the teeth elongating in my mouth, and the claws extending out of my fingertips.

I can feel it all happening in slow motion, and I can feel myself stop the transformation just before I am forced onto all fours.

There I stand, towering over a slack-jawed Ivor. Me, but not me. I am at least 7 feet tall with the extension of my limbs and spine. I'm more wolf than man, but still, I stand on two legs.

"You dare speak to me about thick blood," I yell at him in a gnarled but clear enough voice.

To my surprise, the awestruck Ivor falls to his knees and lowers his head straight to the ground. I spare a glance at Bo to make sure I am not imagining things, and, to my surprise, he lowers himself to the ground while staring at me in amazement. The three PS guards emerging from the tree line, still in their wolf forms and all of them immediately whine and fall to the ground with their bellies in the air.

"Ulfheðnar," Ivor mutters into the ground. Then, in a loud voice, he declares, "The True King revealed."

I see my reflection in the SUV paint. I guess I am a sight to behold in this form. Ivor isn't wrong either, I look a lot like my ancestors, the original Ulfheðnar. Who knew?

Damn, I really look awesome. I'll have to practice this more often. That's a hell of a King I'm looking at. No wonder they fell to their bellies.

Realizing that the battle is won, I let the PS handle Ivor and I turn my attention back to Ellie. I shift back to human form and run to her side. If Ivor is right, I have to give her my blood to save her.

"Bo," I yell, snapping him out of his trance. "Get over here and help me."

Bo runs to my side, and the guards easily handle Janeal and Ivor.

My brother looks pale and shaken, "Bo, she's losing a lot of blood, and there might be damage to her brain. I don't think we have time to get her to a hospital."

Ivor yells to us, "You must give her your blood, King. It is the only way to unleash her wolf form and save her. It was in the prophecy; the True King will set her free."

Bo is shaking his head. "No, Jasper, we can't do it."

"What the fuck do you mean we can't do it," I say. "We can and we will."

"No," he says again. "It's against the treaty."

"Fuck the treaty," I yell. "This is Ellie's life. Who the fuck cares about a treaty?"

"She does," Bo says looking down at the woman who I know he is hopelessly in love with. The woman who almost instantly became like a little sister to me.

I take a breath because I know what he is saying. Ellie lived her whole life upholding the treaties of men. She believes in the system, even after it took her parents. But would she rather die than break the treaty?

I can see the pain in Bo's face.

"Ok," I say to him. "You drive Janeal's car to the hospital, and I will stay in the back with Ellie."

"Don't be stupid," Ivor yells. "You must save her, King. Don't let her suffer another 1,000 years trapped as a pitiful human."

※

Bo is driving like a lunatic, which is fine because I don't want him to see what I'm up to back here.

I know what Bo said, and I know how dedicated Ellie is to her role as an ambassador, but I'll be damned if a single line of text from a century-old treaty is going to stand in the way of me saving my best friend's soul mate.

They can both hate me for the next hundred years, but at least they'll be together. Ellie will be alive. I mean, come on, what brings a couple together better than a common enemy?

I say a silent prayer to Luna before I whisper into Ellie's ear, "I want you to name your firstborn after me. Even if you hate me for this."

Extending a single claw, I slice a neat line into my forearm and another into Ellie's neck. I hold her tight against me, allowing my blood to pump into her veins.

242

For a few terrifying seconds, Ellie seems to get worse. She is pale, and her breathing slows down. I start to wonder if I have killed her, and tears begin to fill my eyes.

Thankfully, as the seconds tick by I can start to see the color coming back to her face. Her breathing gets stronger. Another moment later and her eyes are moving under her eyelids.

Her skin starts to feel warm, like really warm, and she seems to be…glowing.

"Bo," I yell. "Stop the car."

Chapter Thirty-One

Pulling Ellie from the back seat of the car, I lay her in the grass. I have no idea what is happening, and I don't know what I am doing, but it just feels like it's the right thing.

Bo shoves me in the chest, and he is yelling at me. "What the fuck did you do, Jasper?"

"She was going to die, Bo," I say as calmly as I can. I know he is half-crazed with grief and adrenaline, so I don't look directly at him and instead, I keep my eyes on Ellie.

"What's happening?" he says. "Why is she glowing? What did you do to her?"

"She was almost dead, and I gave her my blood," I respond, slowly backing away from Ellie as Bo rushes to her side. "It was a lot of blood, she took a lot of blood, but I think it's working. She is breathing, and her skin is warm again."

I can see that Ellie's eyes are moving fast behind her eyelids, and her chest is rising and falling rapidly with her breath, but nothing else on her body is moving.

"What do we do?" Bo turns to me and asks in a softer tone. When I meet his gaze, I can see the worry in his eyes.

"I don't know," I say honestly. "I guess we wait. Do you think we should still take her to the hospital?"

"I don't know," he answers. "I've never been through this. I don't really know what to expect. I think she would want privacy, but what if she needs help? How long does this take? Is it dangerous to her? What if she still needs her head looked at?"

Bo lifts her head to check on her wounds, only to find that they have completely healed. All that remains are clumps of dried blood in her hair.

I rack my brain trying to remember everything that I have ever been told about the conversion process. Bo and I were both taught about it in school, but it was so long ago, and the information was spotty at best.

"Let's call your dad," I say to Bo. "He's been at this longer than both of us. Maybe he knows someone who has been through this or has even seen it before."

Bo stands to retrieve his phone from his pocket, but before he can make the call, we are both thrown to the ground and blinded by a bright flash of light.

After a second, the light retreats and I can focus my brain again. I realize that I am somehow in my wolf form. I look to where Bo had been standing to see him in his wolf form as well. Instinctively, I try shifting back to my human form, but nothing happens.

"What the fuck is going on?" I casually think to myself aloud in my mind.

"I have no idea," Bo answers me. *IN. MY. MIND.*

"WHAT THE FUCK," we both yell, but inside my head.

"How are you in my head?" Bo yells.

I yell back, "You are in my head, bro."

"You are both correct," a female voice says. "And incorrect."

"Ellie?" we both say almost in unison.

I turn to see the largest white wolf I have ever seen. She is stunning, and her head is adorned with ancient runes. She towers over Bo and me and exudes an otherworldly dominance that I can't even put into words.

I want to stare at her in awe, but I want to lower my head in respect. I've never felt anything like the power she exudes.

"I don't understand," I think-speak to her. "How is Bo in my head, how are you in my head?"

"Again," she says, "you are both correct and incorrect."

"What is happening, Ellie?" Bo pleads for an answer.

"I will answer all of your questions," she says. "Both spoken and unspoken, but you must allow me to provide this information without interruption. You do not need to articulate your thoughts to me, I know what you seek through your emotional impressions."

"I don't understand," Bo says.

"I know you don't," she responds. "But you will. Now, be silent."

Bo and I look at each other, and both sit down in submission to this majestic wolf in front of us. The two strongest alpha wolves in the realm, and here we are like pups in school.

"Your minds are linked together through mine. I am both Ellie and Datura, as well as many others. In this realm, I appear as either a wolf or a human, but neither is my true form. Your misguided prisoner was mostly correct in his beliefs about me and his interpretations of the stories I was able to leave behind in my first human life. I was cursed to forget about my wolf form and my connection to the divine, but not right away. Not even Jehovah is capable of that kind of power. So, he hid me from my mother while I lost my memories gradually over the centuries. During this last lifetime, all I could hold onto was the idea that I was designed to blend in but meant for something more. It was never the intention of my uncle that I be killed or lost to the realms forever, so he made sure that there would be a way to release me from my curse when the time was right. As for why now, and why you, Jasper Adolpha, only Jehovah can answer that. As for your questions about the Ellie you both love so dearly, and what happens next. I don't have that answer either. Ellie is me, and I am her. I have all of her memories and emotions, but also the memories and emotions from all of my previous lives. For now, all I can tell you is that I will be returning to the realm of my mother, and perhaps, I will see you again, but that part is not entirely up to me. Thank you both for releasing me."

Then, before I can even formulate a response, Bo and I are in our human forms again.

Lying in the grass.

Alone.

EPILOGUE:

One Year Later

Datura

"You are watching him again, aren't you?" asks my mother in her best casual tone.

"NO," I say a little too sharply. "I mean, I'm not watching him, I'm just checking in on him. It's a lot to process for a mortal. I just wanted to make sure that he is handling the knowledge of the divine and having been in the presence of a Goddess well. He's a good leader to his people, who are also our people, so it's normal that I check on him."

"It has been a full turn for him," she says. "I am sure he is fine."

I gaze into the reflection pool waters and summon the image of Bo at his desk. He is not fine. In fact, I would say that he's a mess.

"Mother," I say, not looking away from the image. "Look at him. He looks unwell. He hasn't replaced his housemaid, he isn't eating well, his beard is overgrown and unkept, and there are coffee cups everywhere."

My mother shifts her gaze to me. "It is very mortal of you to notice such things."

"Isn't that why you sent me to live among them?" I retort. "I was supposed to learn about them, and I did. Over the years, I lived among the wolves and the humans. Their lives are fragile and fleeting, but they form these strong bonds with each other, and they feel great pain when those bonds are broken."

"So, you watch this mortal because you're the cause of his pain," she asks with a hint of genuine interest in her voice.

The divine race has never thought of the mortals under their care as much more than pets. They use the mortal realms to try to one-up each other. Each one claims their mortal race to be the best.

Ironically, after creating the realms and races, they have mostly ignored them. Most of the divine interference that a realm experiences is at the hands of a jealous sister or brother of their creator. Rarely will a divine being step in and assist their own realms. Some of our lesser cousins will sometimes pop into a realm and cause chaos, but that too is rare.

"He mourns my loss," I say. "Or at least the loss of Ellie. But he also mourns his friend, Janeal. He is hurt by her betrayal. The mortals are sensitive about loyalty. He would have put himself in danger to keep her safe, so it pains him that she was not his true ally. It's hard to describe and even harder to understand."

"Do you mourn him as well?" my mother asks with a confused look on her face.

"Yes," I say honestly. "In all of my mortal lives, no one has forged a connection with me the way he did. I lived each life as a solitary woman, blending into the background and never marrying or having children. Since I was never really a mortal being, I never craved any type of mortal bond. It was only during this last lifetime, as Ellie, that I even considered that I might want to be a part of a mortal family."

After what seems like forever, my mother simply shrugs and replies, "How peculiar."

BO

"There is nothing," Jasper says. "I have been to every single pack library. I've talked to every pack historian. I even met with the asshat Fae Council. No one has any information about the divine realm or how to get to it. It might be time to move on from this, Bo."

Jasper and I have had these conference calls at least three times a week for the past year, and for the last three months, they have been the same. He pleads with me to give up, and I plead with him to keep looking.

So far, I have won every time, but I can hear the resolve in his voice. I know his patience is growing thin with me. I've ignored almost all of my pack business, and I've dominated Jasper's time as well.

"I just need to be sure that she's OK," I say. "I don't have to go there; I just need to get her a message. I just need some sort of sign that she is alive. Besides, I know the humans don't believe our story, and until we get some proof that Ellie is OK, they will always believe that we killed her."

"I miss her too," Jasper says. "But you aren't doing her any favors by wallowing around, ignoring your pack, and living off coffee and stale donuts."

Great, Jasper has been talking to my mother.

"I'm just not ready to give up on her yet," I say in a barely recognizable voice, filled with desperation.

Jasper and my mother aren't wrong. I've let myself go. I've refused to hire a new housekeeper. I barely leave the house and survive off whatever baked goods my mother drops off during her weekly visits.

My council members don't stop by for meetings anymore, and I don't even know if they're still sending me my weekly briefs.

I can't even remember the last time I shifted and went for a run. Maybe that's part of the problem, maybe I'll be able to think better if I shift for a little bit, just an hour or so.

"Come on man," Jasper says in a soft tone, like he is speaking to a child. "What would Ellie say if she saw you like this?"

I can hear someone walking up to my front door. I could have sworn today was Tuesday; mom comes over on Wednesdays. Could it be Wednesday already?

"Hey," I say to Jasper. "What day is it?"

"It's Tuesday, man," he says with pity in his voice.

"That's what I thought," I say, heading towards the front door with my tablet. "I think my mom's here early this week. Better stay on the call so she can say hi."

Reaching the front room, I pull up the door.

It's the scent that smacks me in the face first. Whipping my head up, I drop the tablet to the ground.

"Ellie!"

Jasper

"Really," I yell at the screen in front of me. "The day I tell him to give up, you come to the front door. I'm never going to hear the end of this."

Stay up to date on

the release of

WOLF WALKERS

THE GODDESS

by following me on

TikTok, Instagram, and

YouTube

@jlthompson_author

Pssssttt…Find an error?

Email: jlthompsonauthor@gmail.com

The first person to report each error will be mentioned by name in the acknowledgments of the reprint edition, so be sure to include your full name in the email.

www.ingramcontent.com/pod-product-compliance
Lightning Source LLC
Chambersburg PA
CBHW071555110726
47908CB00007B/2109